PRAISE FROM READERS

"It's very clear from these stories that you're not just a children's writer. You're a writer. And I for one could quite happily read loads more like this. I'm very glad I had the honour of reading them and wish you all the success in the world."
~ Bob Stone, author and owner of Write Blend Bookshop

"Wonderfully evocative, quietly sinister, great intrigue and well written. I'm enjoying the variety and your talent. Just brilliant."
~ J M Moore, author

"The most striking is the Space in Our Days. Very, very clever. It made me think. It's still making me think. This story still haunts me from the first time I ever read it. Truly spectacular."
~Lexi Rees, author.

"This has been an epic journey of laughter, tears, dark moments and spine-chilling adventure. Full of twists and turns, humour and sadness. I think you have covered every human emotion and some very hard-hitting topics as well as the rawness of real life from all perspectives."
~ Cath Roberts, avid reader.

COMPLETE LIST OF JUDE'S BOOKS

The Slow Down for Bobby books
SuperBob
STOP - SuperBob Tells Off Parents

Hal's Books
Hal and the End Street
Hal and the Parties

The Lamby Series
Astronaut Lamby
Floga with Flossie
Pirate Lamby and His Woolly Crew
Lamby goes Camping
Lamby and Flossie's Tales from the Travel Pouch

Other Titles
The Dragon of Allerton Oak
The Toffee Lady
Am I Nearly There Yet?
Glad to be Dan
Fernando Can Tango

Educational books
Little Lamb Phonics - Making Phonics f-u-n

A Slice of Lennon

By
Jude Lennon

Little Lamb Publishing · Little Lamb Publishing · Little Lamb Publishing

A Slice of Lennon

First published in 2019

Copyright © Jude Lennon 2019

The rights of the author have been asserted in accordance with Sections 77 and 78 of the Copyright Designs and Patents Act, 1988.

ISBN: 978-1-9997959-4-8

TEAM AUTHOR UK
Publishing with you

DEDICATION

This book is dedicated to the memory of my mum Carol Lennon. From her, I inherited my love of books and gin. Ironically her order was always for gin with 'ice and **no** slice'.

CONTENTS

ABOUT A SLICE OF LENNON

This collection of stories was inspired by the writing group I'm part of. The group is named 'The Revolting Peasants' after one of our earliest writing prompts. We meet every month to share our work and to give and receive feedback. There is always tea and cake consumption and sometimes even the odd glass of wine.

Each month we choose a theme or writing prompt and set ourselves the challenge of writing 500 (ish) words around it. The 'ish' has a tendency to grow and sometimes by quite a lot. We've used many things to kickstart our writing including photographs, quotes, poems, album covers and random objects. Many, but not all of the stories in this collection have started life following a writing prompt from this group.

Although most of the books I've written to date are picture books for children, being part of this group has allowed my writing pen to wander into the territory of the grown-up audience. I've thoroughly enjoyed the process. Like the writing prompts themselves, this collection is varied in content and theme and I hope I've captured a wide range of human emotions.

Over the years, many people have asked when I was going to publish something for adults, so the answer is - now!

So, if you are about to sit down and enjoy a well-earned gin or other beverage of choice – *A Slice of Lennon* is the perfect accompaniment.

I hope you enjoy...cheers!

UNCLE STEPHEN

Jake stepped out onto the deck and shivered. He'd never known cold like it. Raw, savage and aggressive, it attacked his exposed flesh in seconds. He pulled the zip up on his ridiculously expensive but warm coat. He was thankful he'd allowed Molly to talk him into buying it.

Approaching the railing, he watched as the eerie, icy shapes stared mournfully back at him. Varying shades of grey, black, navy, blue and even white mingled and played tricks with his eyes. People who simply described night as dark or black had never experienced a Norwegian landscape in winter.

Not for the first time, he wondered whether he'd made a mistake. Was searching for his Uncle Stephen a futile expedition? And it was an expedition. They'd been planning the trip for over a year. Simply finding a boat willing to take them through the Fjords at this time of year had taken months. Not for them the luxurious cruises with champagne and dinner at the Captain's table. They were in a small, supply boat, crewed by a group of weather-beaten sailors anxious to get the journey done before the worst of the winter set in. He and Molly would be dropped off at the town of Hedmark before embarking on a day's journey to the remote village of Koensgrad. It would be another two days before they arrived.

And once there, they had very little to go on. His uncle – Stephen Clarke – had been missing for some years. The last confirmed sighting of him was in Hedmark ten years ago.

His mum had begged him to try and find her only brother. They'd been so close when they were younger, and she'd never got over him leaving the country in such haste. As she succumbed to sickness, the begging became her deathbed request. A request that felt increasingly more like a Herculean task, but one he simply couldn't have refused.

The deck door opened and banged to behind him. Turning, he saw Molly heading towards him with two steaming mugs.

'I presumed you wanted it laced.' she said handing over a mug to Jake's waiting hands.

He sipped it gratefully – wow laced it definitely was.

'So, what's the plan when we dock love?' Molly looked up at him with a smile.

This was exactly what Jake had been asking himself since they'd boarded this morning. The ice creaked and re-settled with an ominous sigh. There was something other worldly about the noises coming from the floating land masses. Jake sipped again before turning his back on the icy wilderness.

'We've got to meet up with Sven. He and the other guide Morten are going to take us out on Snowmobiles. I've had to pay extra because of the time of year.'

Molly compressed her lips and tried not to let her eyes roll heavenward. She couldn't really blame Jake; she'd encouraged him to start the expedition in the first place. But as time had gone on, she'd become more aware of the growing costs, fear of failure and the freezing conditions.

'And Sven is sure he took a Stephen Clarke to Koensgard all those years ago?' she asked.

'That's what he said. Stephen Clarke, a British man who spoke Norwegian fluently. I guess there aren't that many of us who speak the language at all, never mind with the fluency of a local. We're a rare breed.'

Molly nodded. Jake's ability to speak Norwegian had been one of the things she'd found so intriguing about him when they first met.

'And once we get to Koensgard?' she persisted.

Until now, every time she'd asked this Jake had evaded answering. And because she loved him and because deep down, she loved adventure she had just gone with the flow. She knew that this kind of planning - the emotional reality of the trip - was better in her hands.

Jake sighed; he didn't know what they'd do once they finally arrived. For so long, the journey itself had occupied every waking hour. Buying the right thermals, getting new passports, finding the boat, making contact with Sven, these had been the things he'd thought about. Now, the destination was getting closer and the reality of WHY he'd actually come on this trip was starting to sink in. He had no plan. No plan at all. He'd dragged Molly out here at the most dangerous time of year, they were in debt up to their eyeballs and he had no plan. What if Uncle Stephen was dead or worse, simply didn't want to be found?

'Molly I honestly don't know. What do you think I should do?'

Sipping the last of her coffee, Molly took hold of Jake's glove covered hand. 'Let's speak to Sven. He's your best bet. He's the one with the local contacts. He's the one who saw him last. We've got the whole afternoon in Hedmark tomorrow. We'll meet him as arranged and make a list of things to ask him. You know how much I love a list.'

Jake enveloped Molly in a padded bear hug and kissed the top of her woolly hat. 'Thanks love. Let's go in, before we die of frostbite.'

Stripping off layers and dabbing at dripping noses, Jake and Molly settled down at the tiny table and chairs in the communal area of the boat. Looking at Jake's tired face, Molly wasn't sure she could contain herself much longer. But she'd made a promise.

She'd been more than surprised when Sven had contacted her directly. The surprise had grown when a sealed envelope had made its way into her rucksack with specific instructions to tell Jake nothing until they met. The rest of the envelope's contents set Molly's mind racing with questions despite filling in some of the missing pieces.

Stephen Clarke had arrived in Hedmark ten years ago in the middle of a blizzard, dripping blood from a couple of nasty wounds that had made pink stepping-stones in the snow. Somehow, he'd dragged himself to one of the out-of-season log cabins in the woods and started his long road to recovery. For the first few days he'd survived on sleep, boiled water and berries. His training had prepared him for this and after a few days, he was strong enough to start hunting in earnest for food. He'd certainly not starved.

As the wounds started to recover, heal and shrink, Stephen Clarke started to disappear too. He was a man in need of a new beginning. A man running from a past that would surely kill him if it caught him. A man who had to be as a dead man to those who loved hm.

There were no specifics about what he'd actually done or the secret agency he might have worked for. Molly couldn't help herself as images of James Bond flashed through her mind. The reality would probably be very different! For all she knew, Stephen was a violent criminal who'd committed murder and other kinds of atrocities. Better to think of him as a glamorous spy with fast cars and gadgets. She couldn't repress a shiver of excitement.

Her sense of excitement quickly changed to one of apprehension. Molly wasn't sure how Jake would take the news about this much-loved Uncle. He'd been placed on a pedestal and revered as one would a demi-god. The fall from grace could be pretty spectacular. All she could do was be there when Sven made his findings known. She knew that the final disclosure would be the most shocking of all for Jake to accept. Stephen Clarke no longer existed but Sven Klokk did.

CUT AND BLOW

Love can be many things.

Annabelle had learnt that over the last six months. When her boss had first explained the new role she had in mind for her, Annabelle had wanted to run screaming from the salon and never return.

Tina had always had it in for her. Since her first day as a newly trained hairdresser, Tina had gone out of her way to belittle her and put her down. Only the presence of Kaya the other stylist kept her put.

'Ignore her. She's just got a chip on her shoulder the size of a King Edward. She was the same with me at first.'

'Yes, but I've been here for three years now and it's not getting any better.' Annabelle swept the remaining clumps of hair together with vigour.

'Bottom line babes, she's jealous. Jealous of anyone younger than her and jealous of anyone who can offer the customers more than a shampoo and set or French Pleat. She's only hanging onto this place until she retires and then it will be mine. And things will be very different then, believe me!'

And Annabelle did believe her. She'd never seen anyone with such untameable confidence as Kaya.

The day after this conversation, Tina dropped the bombshell.

'Annabelle, a word please.'

Swallowing nervously, Annabelle headed into the back room frantically wondering what she'd done now.

'New initiative for salons to do more for the community. One afternoon a week you'll be offering hairdressing services at the Homeless Shelter. You start tomorrow. Here's the address. That's all.'

Stunned, Annabelle accepted the piece of paper held out to her and left the room in a daze.

The Homeless Shelter? Ashamed to admit it, she hadn't even known where it was until she'd read the address. Sure, she'd seen the homeless asleep on the streets. Who hadn't? Their numbers were multiplying on a weekly basis, sleeping in doorways clutching ragged quilts and torn sleeping bags to their filthy bodies. And it wasn't like she didn't care. She'd dropped bags of unwanted clothes to the collection point set up before Christmas and she'd left the occasional cup of tea or sandwich next to a malodorous form as she passed by. But she'd never thought of offering real, tangible help. Tina had done this on purpose!

The next day, Annabelle arrived at the shelter and the smell enveloped her from the door. Unwashed hair, unwashed clothes, unwashed bodies. She could feel her lunch struggling to stay put. Taking a breath, she crossed the hall past a row of slumped figures, a sea of faces all chiselled with despair.

'You must be Annabelle.' A tall man with a well-trimmed beard greeted her. His luxuriantly wavy hair fell just below his ears in a style that looked 'just out of bed' but in reality, probably took hours to perfect.

'Good of you to come. I'm Sam by the way. We've set up a hairdressing corner over here. You ok to start on the back wash?'

It was like being back in training thought Annabelle. Washing hair with care was the first thing she'd learned. Rolling up her sleeves Annabelle beckoned to the next person in line.

The man stood up with difficulty and made his way slowly and painfully across. He half fell into the chair, pulling and plucking nervously at the edge of his filthy coat. Making sure the water was the right temperature, she gently draped the man in a gown, eased him back in the chair and started. As the hot water made contact with the dirty matted hair the rising odour was eye watering. Annabelle hoped she wouldn't gag.

Rivulets of grime, muck and grease joined the clear stream and danced their murky way down the plughole. Annabelle applied some shampoo and the man flinched. She gently rubbed the shampoo through his hair and then massaged his scalp. As always, she took extra care around the ears and neck. The man's hands clenched tightly as her fingers rubbed and scrubbed the dirt away. When she applied the second dollop of shampoo, he seemed to relax. His fingers loosened and he looked almost at peace. The faintest smile was pulling at the corners of his chapped lips. As she rinsed the bubbles away, Annabelle noticed tears running from the man's closed eyes.

'Are you ok?' she asked gently.

'Just grand. Yours are the first hands to touch me with any kindness in years. I'd just forgotten what it was like.'

'What's your name?' Annabelle asked while combing conditioner through the now squeaky-clean hair.

'William, but everyone calls me Bill.'

'Well Bill, why don't you tell me a bit about yourself...'

* * *

Annabelle made a point of asking every single person about themselves. Surprisingly, most people were only too pleased to talk. They all had their own stories to tell. Tales of bereavement, lost jobs, troubled home lives, mental health struggles, drug addiction, abuse, bloody awful bad luck. The reasons for living on the streets were many and varied. What wasn't many and varied was how everyone looked - old and tired. Even the youngest people were craggy faced and stooped over. They were aged before their time.

For six months Annabelle had been washing, cutting, brushing and styling the hair of the homeless. Just like the salon, some of the people came once and never returned. Others, like Bill, were regulars and she came to see them just as she did her regular clients back at Tina's. Other than holiday plans and TV, the topics of conversation were pretty similar – politics, weather, human interactions. Funny how a role she once thought she'd loath had come to be the highlight of her week.

Her and Sam got on well too. Really well in fact. She didn't want to get carried away, but he seemed like a keeper. But that relationship was merely the icing. The real cherries were the interactions with the people who came to the shelter. The expressions on people's faces when her and Sam had finished were priceless.

'That can't be me!' was the frequent cry.

Shock, disbelief, overwhelm, tears, smiles and laughter were all reflected back from the mirror. They stood taller, they looked younger, they seemed more confident. That little bit of love was vital to them.

'I don't think you and Sam realise what you've done,' Bill said one day as she smoothed styling products onto his freshly cut hair.

'You've given us what we all crave – kindness, touch, warmth, acceptance and love. You've made us human again. You've made us worthwhile.'

Bill shrugged himself into his battered coat and Annabelle moved on impulse. Stretching out, she put her arms around Bill and hugged him to her, dirty coat and all.

The smell of coconut styling products and Annabelle's perfume mixed with the fuggy, stale grime of the streets and swirled around them both. Bill's initial shock at this unexpected gesture prevented him from moving but after a moment he returned the hug. Feeling tears rising, he dropped his arms and stepped back.

'See you next week for my usual appointment.'

And with a brief smile he was at the door and back into the city where he was nobody once more.

CHANGES

'For goodness sakes John, I'm only dancing! What is your problem?' I yelled over the top of the music.

'Only dancing! Gyrating and making a fool of yourself more like. It's not what people expect from a woman in your position.'

A woman in my position? Ugh! I continued to dance unabashed. As the track ended, I turned and made my way off the dance floor. It was time to go. I couldn't stay in this suffocating, life draining room a minute longer.

As I bent to pick up my coat, it dawned on me that I couldn't leave. I, of all people, had to be here. My speech would go down in history as a rebel yell. Stifling a sigh, I moved to a nearby table and sat down.

'How is everyone enjoying the evening?' I enquired.

A chorus of 'marvellous thanks' reached out across the crisp white cloth and plates of food. This is what you'd call a lovely traditional spread. Cold-meats, perfectly filled and cut sandwiches, sausage rolls – homemade of course. All prepared by the long-suffering wives and girlfriends of the village of Pankurst.

Admittedly, for some of the wives, spending hours making perfect pastry was their idea of heaven. Most of them, however, did it through gritted teeth. The same teeth that clenched with annoyance when the team football kits arrived home and awaited the work of the magic washing fairy. I had avoided this fate wherever I'd called home and had even managed to introduce my own not so subtle changes to more than one antiquated village.

I'd decided that Pankurst was in need of my help some months previously and tonight would see the labours of our hard work.

Janine and Tanika had been the first two converts and it hadn't exactly been difficult to get them on board.

'Oh, I love it!' said Tanika, her eyes shining. 'It's definitely time for change around here. Count us in.'

Next on the list, Simona and Katya.

'If it works it will be amazing! I'm sick of being expected to wash the kits and make bloody sausage rolls.' Simona enthused.

To be fair I couldn't imagine the feisty Simona being expected to do anything, but it was good to have her support.

The plotting and planning had continued. Janine and Tanika worked on the playground mums. Simona dropped subtle hints at her Art classes. Katya handed out leaflets at her Yoga sessions. Most of the women in the village had taken to the plans with enthusiasm. The only ones left to convince were the 'Old Guard' at the Cygnet Committee.

The WI meeting seemed like the perfect chance to put forward my proposals. I knew there could be some resistance; Margery, Philippa and Carol were avid pastry makers and martyrs to the cause of sausage rolls. They also maintained the outmoded view that men should be fussed over and couldn't be trusted to boil a kettle never mind anything else. I only hoped the others would back me up when push came to shove.

As the guest speaker was thanked by the Chair Jean (or Jeanie as we all called her), I made eye contact with my allies around the table. The moment was here.

'Any other business before tea and cake?' asked Jeanie.

'I'd like to say a few words if I may. I have some interesting ideas and proposals to put to you all for the next Village Dance.

'Very well, what would you like to suggest?' Jeanie gave a tight smile.

Taking a deep breath, I jumped straight in. The ideas from the previous few months were shared in a dynamic five-minute segment duly noted by Doreen who was keeping the minutes. As my presentation gathered pace, I became aware of Jeanie, Margery, Carol and Philippa looking at me. First with disbelief, then wonder and finally with a definite seal of approval. Doreen almost forgot to write.

'So, what do you think ladies?' I asked nervously.

'They'll hate it!' said Philippa.

'Good,' said Jeanie 'It's about time their cosy little world was shaken a little. I for one will be quite happy to sit and enjoy myself for once. Make a note Doreen, motion passed.'

I'll be honest, I hadn't expected that! I'd been prepared for disbelief and outright hostility. This emphatic acceptance had come as a shock.

'Thank you, ladies. I'll have all the final arrangements in place by the next meeting,' I promised.

With an air of self-congratulation, I made my way home to LeeRoy. As I wandered over and gave him a kiss, he looked at me with a knowing twinkle in his eye.

'Out with it! What are you planning this time?'

'Moi, little old moi?' I batted my eyelashes.

'Up to your old tricks I suppose. The poor villagers won't know what's hit them.' He sighed before returning to his crossword puzzle.

'Oh, only half the village dear.'

LeeRoy smiled as I sat down and kicked off my shoes.

* * *

And so we return to the night where this story began – The Village Dance. Traditionally the women spent the day decorating the hall, ironing tablecloths, making the buffet and generally ensuring that the men's comfort was of paramount importance.

I'd kicked back against such outdated activities since taking up my vocation ten years previously. Wherever we'd lived I'd managed to bring about changes that were for the better of the community. LeeRoy had become accustomed to the moving that came with the territory and he'd always been fully supportive. Enjoying the 'ring side seat at the show' as he put it. He was looking forward to tonight's show too.

It was time for my speech and dreary John welcomed me forward to the microphone. Taking a steadying breath, I began.

'It gives me great pleasure to thank you all for attending this wonderful event. These quarterly dances are the highlight of Pankurst's busy social calendar. A way to bring us all together and raise some much-needed funds for our local teams. As you know, our committee work tirelessly to keep everything going. So tirelessly that we've decided to change a few things.' I cleared my throat.

''From now on there will be a women's football team. In accordance with the new guidelines, the men's and women's teams will be responsible for their own kit which must be washed and dried by team members only!' A few splutters accompanied this, but I carried on regardless.

'The Village dance will no longer be catered for solely by the women of Pankurst. Quite frankly they have had enough and think it's time the men took care of their own sausage rolls. The golden years of being mollycoddled and fussed over are on their way out!' More splutters and a few expletives too.

'The tablecloths for the Village dance will no longer be the responsibility of the women of Pankurst. There is an iron and ironing board in the cupboard here. Please make use of them.' Even more splutters, and definitely more expletives.

'Dancing, particularly gyrating, making fools of ourselves and generally having a good time will be actively encouraged. There'll even be dancing in the streets if we feel like it.' Silence from one half of the room, whoops from the other.

'From now on the women of Pankurst refuse to live in some kind of Stepford Wives movie and instead will be embracing classes including Electronics, Car Maintenance, DIY and Shed Building.' Silence was overcome by cheers.

I became aware of John hurrying onto the stage with a determined look on his face. He lunged for the microphone with a look of savagery that the Middle England gloss couldn't hide.

'Give that microphone here! This is an outrage! I'll report you to the highest orders,' he spat the words between his teeth.

'Steady on John, surely, you don't want to hurt a woman of the cloth.' I gave him my best lipstick smile.

John recalled himself. The room was looking on with interest, speculation and unease.

'Well Vicar, I'm sure we can talk about this at our next meeting. Shall we get back to the dance for now.' John could barely contain his irritation but was giving it his best shot.

Laying a firmer hold on the microphone, I addressed the room again.

'All those in favour of a more equal, fair, considerate Pankurst raise your glass.'

The women's glasses were raised with a vigour that sent gin, wine and Pimms sloshing dangerously close to the rims. Some of the men were quick to join them raising assorted mixtures of wine, beer and whiskey to show their support. Others scanned the room before slowly committing themselves to the most exciting thing to have happened in Pankurst for years. The villagers had voted and only a small group of unsmiling men kept their drinks firmly on the tables. No doubt they'd drown their sorrow later.

'Well I'd say that's pretty much decided, wouldn't you? Here's to a new Pankurst!'

As John left the room in what I can only describe as an epic strop, LeeRoy led me to the dance floor.

'I know this one's your favourite,' he grinned. 'Let's dance, Vicar.'

And we did!

For the Bowie fans amongst you, the prompt for this piece was his album Changes. The brief was simple, use one, some or any Bowie song titles as inspiration. The songs didn't even have to be from the album. I used ten, did you spot them all? Answers below...

John I'm Only Dancing

Rebel Rebel (admittedly this was referred to as the rebel yell)

Changes

Janine

Cygnet Committee

Gene Genie (or Jeanie as she's called in the story)

Golden Years

Dancing in the Streets

Sorrow

Let's Dance

A TASTE OF FREEDOM

'Damned peasants,' hissed Gilbert de Aston slamming his fist onto the table. 'Who do they think they are?'

His wife Matilda lowered her eyes and said nothing.

An uprising had started in the next county and was showing signs of spreading quicker than the Peasants Revolt which had shaken the population some thirty years earlier. Matilda had some sympathy, nay, empathy with them. She was little more than a serf herself. Sold in matrimony to the man who'd bedazzled her father – and her.

Oh, Gilbert had made the right noises during the wooing. Above average height with a mane of tawny coloured hair, Gilbert had made many a maiden's heart flutter. Matilda had been flattered when he had singled her out as the object of his gallantry. He had written her beautiful poetry and whispered sweet nothings on his visits to her father's lands. When she'd accompanied her father on a return-journey to his castle, he had shown nothing but care and consideration – a regular Troubador. He'd beguiled them both.

No sooner had the priest tied the knot than Gilbert's true nature had surfaced. The true nature that the tenants on his land, the local gentry and his servants had been well aware of. Matilda now knew why he had sought the hand of a lady from the other side of the country. Since the wedding day, she had learnt to hold her tongue, lower her eyes and suffer in silence. Gilbert's soft caresses were soft no more. Harsh words accompanied harsh fists. Forbidden to write to her father unless Gilbert read the letters and forbidden to leave the castle unless Gilbert accompanied her, she felt fettered and tethered. Her freedom curtailed by a band of gold and precious stones.

'Damn these peasants to hell!' Gilbert snarled. 'I must leave tonight to suppress this unruly mob.'

'Yes, my lord. Shall I help you prepare for the journey?' Matilda asked cautiously.

'No, I want none of your chattering distraction. Go and order the kitchen to prepare my supplies. And then, keep out of my way woman!'

Matilda stood, curtseyed, and left the room.

* * *

How quiet and calm the castle seemed without Gilbert. Matilda and her maid Sybilla occupied themselves with needle and thread in the solar. The monotony of setting stitches allowed Matilda time to think.

She imagined the sight of the peasants in revolt. Some clutching pitchforks, some with cudgels and sticks. She could hear them too. Their feet marching ever closer, gathering followers at every hamlet and village they passed. Onwards they marched...beating a path to the landed lords.

Matilda became aware of hurried feet on the stone staircase. Looking up, Raymond, the castle steward, burst through the door.

'My lady, forgive me, but the peasants are on the march. They're heading towards Lacy Castle.'

Lacy Castle was the largest and wealthiest manor in the area, far bigger than Gilbert's modest family seat. It was also their nearest neighbour and a prime target for those on the march. Even through her own thick walls, there was no mistaking the very real sound of a body of people on the move and getting closer. Matilda felt a jolt of fear which quickly turned to envy, anticipation and excitement.

'Tell the men to ride out to the castle boundary. They may carry arms but are to do nothing unless I say so. You may go

Raymond.' Raymond bobbed his head and left the room in haste.

'Sybilla, quickly bring me your spare gown.' Matilda's eyes shone.

'My lady?' gasped Sybilla

'Now Sybilla, bring it now!'

Her stitch-work lay forgotten on the rushes beneath her feet. She paced the solar nibbling the edges of her fingers. Could she really do this? Was she brave enough? When Sybilla returned she commanded the maid to undress her. Flinging her own silken gown on the floor, she scrambled into a weeping Sybilla's plain woollen one. Finally, she pulled an ugly covering over her hair and headed for the castle entrance.

At the threshold, Matilda faltered before picking up her skirts and running across the bailey and through the gate. This was the first time she'd left the castle unaccompanied since her marriage! As she ran, she heard the unmistakable cry: 'Set us free! Set us free!'

Matilda joined the sea of people who were skirting Gilbert's land. Taking up their rhythm she marched and chanted with them until she had no voice.

'Set me free,' she continued until her voice was hoarse. 'Please set me free.'

Those she walked with were so different from her own station in life. These were people who struggled to feed their families and worried how they would meet the next cruel demand for taxes to fill the rich men's coffers. And yet, here, amongst these people who were fighting so fiercely for their rights, who would probably have torn her apart had they suspected her true identity, she felt safe and secure.

'Set me free! Set me free!' her cry continued, though at a whisper.

Her delicate shoes were torn to shreds and a small stone had wriggled its way between her toes. Moving to the edge of the road she sank down to remove it. And as she sat, crushing realisation hit her. This was futile. Matilda stood up and let the peasants stream past her.

No longer able to accompany them, she glanced behind her and realised she wasn't far from the river where Gilbert had spoken such courtly love to her all those months ago. Not knowing what else to do, she followed the path down to the riverbank.

Breathing in the damp air, she absorbed every detail like a starving animal. The glint of the sun through the trees as it caught on the bubbling water was entrancing. The fish darted between the rocks and boulders on the riverbed and continued unchecked on their way.

Matilda sank down on the grass and allowed the tranquillity of the moment to wash over her. She couldn't help but wonder how it would feel if she too were a fish, free to swim away wherever she chose.

As her gaze followed the fish down the river a leaf fell gently from one of the overhanging trees. It caressed her forehead and cheek the way Gilbert's fingers had once done. Then, all she'd dreamt of was being married to a man who would look after her and cherish her. Gilbert had seemed so perfect and she had revelled in every second she was in his company. Now she dreamt just as ardently about being as far away from him as possible.

During the first few months of their marriage she had looked earnestly for a glimpse of the man he had initially shown her. Surely something could be salvaged, something could be made good of this union. Matilda had searched in vain.

A moorhen bobbing down the river caught her attention and she became aware of a growing chill in the air. The hours of freedom were slipping by and she knew it was time to return to the marriage bonds. After all, she had nowhere else to go. She was a chattel, owned goods.

Standing up and shaking her borrowed skirts free of grass, she turned her back on the river and made her way up onto the path. The dust from hundreds of tramping feet had settled, and there was no sign of life. If it weren't for the far-off cries of: 'set us free!' you would swear nobody had passed that way at all.

She set her shoulders and slowly made her way back to the castle. The contrast between her earlier, confident, jaunty stride and the slow lagging steps she used now were as stark as night and day. As she walked, she took in the landscape, the rolling fields and the smell of freedom. Hot tears coursed down her cheeks.

Creeping back unseen across the bailey, she slipped inside and ran up the stairs to her chamber. Stripping off Sybilla's gown she dressed herself in silk once more. The material floated over her body like air. The ugly covering on her head was discarded in favour of the delicate hair veil she usually wore.

She sat in her chair by the fire, picked up her needlework and with hands that shook, started to sew.

Her chains and fetters were back in place.

Outside she could still hear the distant cry: 'Set us free!'

Historical Note–

The Peasants Revolt took place in 1381 and was the result of years of economic hardship dating from the Black Death (Plague) of the 1340s and the introduction of high taxes. Across rural society, peasants, serfs, artisans and even village officials rose up in protest. They sought an end to serfdom and a reduction in taxes which was initially granted by King Richard II. However, the rebels continued to protest and London came under attack. During this time rebel leader Wat Tyler was killed and the King tried to restore order to the capital. He overturned his earlier decision to reduce taxes and end serfdom.

CIVILISED OUTRAGE

Joanna took a deep breath, taking in the fresh air with a grateful gasp. She left the small, unassuming building on Prinsengracht with an array of emotions fighting for dominance.

Never had a museum affected her this way. The plight of Anne Frank had touched her since she was a child. She remembered devouring each page of her heart-breaking and poignant diary. She'd watched various TV adaptations seeing lives less fortunate than hers played out in glorious technicolour. And she'd heard Otto Frank, Anne's father, describing the horror with wide eyes. A tragic waste of youth, life and talent.

Despite this, she still hadn't been prepared for the reality of the Annexe. Making her way around the rooms, seeing how two families plus another man had lived together in forced intimacy, was a very different experience. She couldn't begin to imagine what they'd been through on a daily basis. Unable to walk around the streets, ride a bike or even flush the toilet. Simple things. Hum drum things. Things people had done without a second thought until the whim of one man's warped ideology said otherwise.

Segregation became the order of the day. People forced to flee, hide or die just because of their religious beliefs. This seemed so alien to Joanna. Her life experience was so different.

But was it? She recalled the news of late, full of images and footage of refugee children clinging to boats with terrified parents. Like Anne's family, they were willing to make sacrifices, even risk their lives for a small chance of survival.

In a daze, Joanna wandered over to the canal to reflect on what she'd seen. She felt inspired and compelled to do something. It was too late for Anne, but maybe she could help others. She could help the modern-day victims of segregation and persecution.

She vowed to get in touch with The Red Cross or Medicine Frontier when she got back to her cosy life in the UK. She'd sign petitions, do some fundraising, volunteer. The possibilities were endless. She WOULD make a difference.

Gradually the bustle of 21st Century Amsterdam filtered back into her senses. The canal water reflected the busy streets and the ring of bicycle bells, car horns and tram warnings brought her back to awareness with a jolt.

She was only here for a weekend and there were still lots of sights to see. Putting her new copy of Anne's diary into her bag, she pulled out the tourist map...ah yes, the Ryksmuseum, a must for any visitor. Stowing the map back in her bag, Joanna set off with a determined step. And with each step, Anne receded from her mind.

THE GINCIDENT

'Gincident – an event or activity (normally stupid) that occurs when too much gin is consumed'.

I was no stranger to them; I'd danced on too many tables, kissed too many unsuitable men, sung truly dreadful karaoke and streaked across the local bowling green whilst in the throes of many a gincident.

And the person at my side on those occasions was Milly. I don't remember a time when I didn't know Milly. We'd met at the playdough table at Toddler Group and had been firm friends ever since.

We'd learnt to read together, to swim together and as we got older to roll joints together. University hadn't got in the way of our friendship; we'd simply picked up the pieces during the holidays. Boyfriends had come and gone but the two of us remained constant.

Ah yes boyfriends. Whereas Milly had a talent for picking 'nice' young men who cherished her but didn't light the flames of passion, I was the original attractor of the bad boy.

'Why oh, why can't I find a decent bloke?' I'd weep for the millionth time. Milly always had the foresight to remove my Bombay Sapphire before it was ruined by salty snot. She really should have bought shares in Kleenex.

So, no one was more surprised than me when I met Pete. He was so different. Funny, witty and caring. Ok, so he didn't give me the thrill I'd got when dating the edgier guys of the past but neither did he scare me with what he might get involved in next. I knew I'd never be called on to pick him up from the local police station after a brawl in a nightclub.

Even better he wasn't in the least bit threatened by my friendship with Milly. More than one relationship had ended because the current Neanderthal had been unwilling to accept that Milly and I were a package.

Initially, Pete and Milly had eyed each other warily but soon warmed to each other.

'Finally, a guy I can have a conversation with! He's a keeper. Just don't go getting any ideas that he's "too nice"!' Milly enthused.

'She's cool, I like her,' had been Pete's verdict.

And so the next few years passed by in a blur of house buying, choosing a puppy (named Scragg), holidays, and domestic chugging along. And then the inevitable wedding to plan and of course, the hen do.

'Leave everything to me!' Milly enthused. 'I know exactly how we'll have the best hen do...nothing tacky I promise.'

She was right. We'd hired a lodge in an upmarket chalet park with a hot tub and fridge stocked with Champagne, wine and of course, gin.

Six giggling women sat in the bubbles under a starlit sky chatting about everything from Bake Off to pert bottoms (or lack of).

'So, what's the most unusual tattoo you've ever seen?' asked Cara. She was a friend from Uni who was well and truly enjoying a weekend away from nappies and runny noses.

I gave a little smirk to myself. Pete's tattoo had been a complete surprise. Mainly because he didn't look like the kind of man to have a tattoo in the first place but also because he certainly didn't look like the kind of man to have a tattoo of a purple unicorn on his inner thigh.

Pulling my mind back from Pete's inner thigh I realised Milly was talking.

'Strangest thing I've ever seen in my life. I mean what kind of man has a purple unicorn on his inner thigh? That was it as far as I was concerned; I wouldn't be going back for more if you know what I mean ladies.'

As I looked up at Milly, I realised she was so fully immersed in her 'gincident' she had no real knowledge of what she'd said or done. She certainly didn't realise she'd given herself and Pete away.

The other girls were laughing uncontrollably but, unable to sit in this oversized bath with drunken women I clambered out, plunged into the cool night air and legged it into the lodge.

Pete, I could almost think about forgiving. My past experience of men had taught me to have low expectations. But Milly! What the hell had she been thinking? We were closer than blood. Rage, shock but mostly disappointment coursed through my now shivering body.

I allowed my breathing and racing heart to steady. I needed to think and think rationally. What were the options? Well, there was the outside chance that there was another bloke running around our town with a purple unicorn tattoo on his inner thigh. Deep down I knew that this was as unlikely as the unicorns themselves. It was also entirely possible that Milly and Pete's gincident had occurred long before I met him. Maybe so much gin had been consumed they could barely remember it. Or, and this was the most depressing of them all, they'd simply been unable to stop themselves.

Any of the options would require me to ask questions and listen to explanations I didn't want to hear. And any of the options would also force me to face the fact that my husband-to-be had slept with my best friend. I shuddered.

Either way, I was faced with the toughest decision of my life – walk away from Pete, walk away from Milly or pretend I'd never heard.

I reached for the gin...

TRUE COST

Surely this was one of the most beautiful beaches in the world; a sickle of near white softness lapped by blue green water. As the sun sank lower in the sky, its warm colours blended and merged to create a peachy pink glow that caressed the sand. The heat of the day was fading too. A slight chill filled the air along with a feeling of anticipation.

For centuries, female turtles had arrived en masse at this secluded spot. They heaved their awkward, ungainly bodies from the turquoise water onto the land. A real labour of love, they dragged themselves slowly from the spray, scaled sloping sands and prepared to nest and lay. Then, their job complete, they returned to the ocean leaving their eggs to the wheel of fortune. Each survivor was a little miracle.

This year would be different. This year the beach waited for the usual influx. It didn't come.

The waves rolled in depositing straws, plastic bottles and carrier bags on the growing shoreline of rubbish. The once beautiful white sand had become a rainbow of chemically enhanced colours. They overpowered the natural beauty around them. Mother Nature was cowed.

The last flickers of sunlight disappeared over the horizon and it was then that she arrived.

The journey had taken longer than last year which had taken longer than the year before. She had struggled through the waters filled with an enemy that was silent but deadly and eventually she had been snared.

Four plastic loops had snatched at her flipper then twisted, turned, caught and held. They tightened as she swam, digging in ever deeper. Tired as she was, she kept going. From time to time the loops would catch on some other alien thing that had claimed the once turquoise waters. The loops tangled with these aliens and tightened further. The flipper could barely move.

Onwards she swam until at last, the beach was in sight. She was exhausted. With great effort she emerged from the water and pulled herself up through the tide line of human selfishness. Gathering her depleting strength, she forged onwards, up through the soft sand and finally found a suitable spot. She had to rest but not for long. More energy required as she scooped and flattened until at last, her nest was ready.

And there, under the moon which highlighted the beauty and ugliness of the place, she laid a perfect white egg. Her job done, she stayed only to cover it with sand before returning painfully to the sea.

The waves took her weight and welcomed her in. But the plastic came too – jostling, bumping, taunting. Her strength was waning as she swam further out. She'd done what she needed to do, and she could do no more.

Her bound flipper hung uselessly at her side. Her eyes were dull and cloudy. With a last gasp she sank motionless to the ocean floor.

Up on the sand a lone turtle egg waited to hatch.

DARK!

Everything was dark.

The walls, the ceiling, the floors and the doors. Funny, how despite the dark, the eye distinguishes the palette of shades and tones from pale grey to pitch black. A full spectrum of non-colour.

Crawling to the door, I grabbed the handle and pulled myself upright. I planted my feet solidly then tugged and heaved with all my might. The door remained firmly shut.

I stretched up on tiptoe and ran my fingers around the top of the doorframe. I'd performed this action a thousand times before and a thousand times had always found what my fingers sought. But not this time. This time, the very thing I was looking for was not there.

Who had moved it? It had always been there. Gran made a point of telling us all where the key was. So much so, that Dad and I suspected she told anyone who visited regardless of how well or little she knew them. She'd always been so trusting.

So, where the hell was it? Was there anywhere else she might have put it? Picking my way carefully around the room, I found myself in front of the piece of furniture that Gran had only ever called 'The Bureau'. An old piece with sturdy legs, three drawers and a drop-down cupboard at the top which when pulled down, transformed it into a writing desk. This was the place where Gran kept all her paperwork and the other things that she had never found a home for.

Turning the small key in the top cupboard, I lowered it down to reveal the contents. The dark took on paler, ghostly grey shades as the bundles of papers made themselves known. Running my fingers through them I knew they didn't have what I was looking for.

Next, I turned my attention to the drawers. I pulled at the top one (always full to the brim) and quickly rifled through the contents. Pushing papers, pens, a hearing aid and a pristine hanky aside – that's when I found it!

The square box with the dragon engraved on the lid brought back a flood of memories. I'd played with it often during my childhood. First keeping buttons in it then pebbles and shells. 'My treasure' Gran had always called it. Wondering what was still inside, I prised off the lid and despite the dark was brought up short by the flash of a diamond. This time, the thing I was looking for was definitely here.

This was the ring Gran had said would be mine. 'Worth a tidy bit,' she'd always said.

I slipped it onto my finger, it had always fitted perfectly. I replaced the box lid and put it back inside the drawer. The rest of the family might choose to disown me, but Gran never would have. It was only fair I should take what was rightfully mine. A keepsake of memories gone by.

There was no need to get through the locked door to the other part of the house now. I'd got what I'd come for. Turning away from the bureau I knew this was the last time I'd come here.

Stepping over the old lady lying on the floor, I pulled the patio door behind me with a familiar and homely click. Good old Gran; I would miss her.

TIGHTS AND OTHER DRAMAS

I was having a bad day! So far, I'd fallen over my tights, banged my nose, cracked my head and twisted my knee.

Things like this weren't supposed to happen to me. I was the 'go to' person in times of strife. Adults and children alike raised their eyes to the sky and pleaded for me to hear. And I did. Swooping in and saving the day was the first thing on my CV under 'additional skills'.

Broken cars – no problem. Burning buildings – a walk in the park. Fighting off villains – bring it on! I laughed in the face of danger. But not today. Today had not gone to plan.

I'd been enjoying some down time during the UK conference I was obliged to attend every year. A flurry of capes, webs, superhero paraphernalia and corresponding superheroes were holed up in an out- of-the-way location for three days every April. This year's hotel was in the archetypal rolling English countryside that those of us who live Stateside adore so much. Enjoying a rare few hours off, a simple walk in the country had almost proved too much for me. The weather was glorious and the winding lane picturesque. You know the kind of thing, hedgerows full of foxgloves, birds and field mice. Idyllic.

The whirring tractor was the only thing to spoil the peace. But even that was hypnotic as the tractor made its way in steady lines up and down the field. The monotony of the noise was comforting and strangely calming. But that all changed when the whirring had taken on a somewhat menacing sound. Something had clanked, banged and popped. Peering over the top of the hedgerow I saw the tractor upended on its side. The farmer appeared to be stuck inside.

There was no time for delay. Looking around for somewhere I could change, I spotted a relic from the past. A quaint red phone box – a rarity on the British landscape these days. It had been many years since I'd used one of these.

Grasping the handle, I heaved the door open and was instantly overwhelmed by the stench of stale urine which had soaked into the ancient concrete floor. The confined space was overflowing with conversations from another time. Conversations of love, anger and frustration clung to the board like business cards advertising ladies of the night.

I drew in a last gasp of fresh air before closing the door. With little time, I started to change and that's when the problem occurred. I cursed the person who had decided that tights were the essential accessory for any self-respecting superhero as my toe caught and my head, nose and knee made contact with phone, door and floor in an appalling piece of choreography.

Scrabbling for both my dignity and clothes I pushed frantically at the door whilst attempting to pull the traitorous 70 Denier up over my knees.

A clunk, whirr and flash assaulted my senses and looking up I saw my nemesis.

There she stood in her fabulous outfit, not a hair out of place, competence at the ready. Casually shaking the Polaroid of embarrassment, Wonder Woman looked me straight in the eye.

'I think you'll find this one is mine, don't you?'

Looking at the emerging image on the photograph I had no choice but to agree. After all, no one wants to see Superman with his tights around his ankles.

THE LINCOLN PENNY

This story is set in 2009

The money box sat on top of the little wooden chest, just as it had always done. The difference now was in the house itself. We'd left it as long as possible, but it couldn't be left any longer. It needed clearing. Aunt Josephine had been a hoarder. Jealously guarding anything that others would have long since discarded. Her cut glass accent reprimanding any who dared to call it 'rubbish'.

Today it was my turn to chip in and I'd taken on the task of the dining room, although we'd only ever known it as Aunt Josie's Parlour.

The money box had always intrigued me. Made of pewter and fashioned into the shape of a Merry Go Round, I'd spent hours tracing the manes and tails of the bobbing horses with my fingers.

As I had done on so many previous visits to the house, I stroked the horses with my fingertip, picked up the box and shook it. Normally the shake was silent, so no one was more surprised than I when a dull and somewhat muffled clunk came from within.

Upending the box, I removed the trap door and shook out the contents. A piece of paper folded over many times landed on the chest. I moved to the dining table and sat down to unwrap the treasure.

Inside was a shiny American cent and the wrapping was in fact a letter addressed to me.

Dearest Beth,

I knew you'd be the one to find this letter and it is right that you now become the guardian of my secret. This knowledge has damn near drowned me all my life which is beautifully ironic as it turns out.

I know you always assumed that your Great Great Grandparents were my mother and father, but nothing could be further from the truth. I am a cuckoo in the nest my dear. I'm not even British although my accent and love of tea would convince you otherwise.

I was born in Virginia, America in 1909 to a serving maid who had got into 'trouble' as they affectionately called it. Why not call it by its real name – rape! The master of the house not wishing to burden his wife with yet another child which would interrupt their pleasure-seeking lives, chose to burden a poor wench from below stairs instead.

I suppose she was luckier than some. My father gave her a Lincoln Penny on a chain as a good luck gift, and they even allowed her to stay. The wife turned a blind eye to the husband's misdemeanours and my mother Mary was promoted to the position of nursery maid to the children of the house. The master and mistress continued their life of pleasure.

Like many other American socialites of the time, they travelled to Southampton, England to board what was billed as the most luxurious and safest ship ever built. Unsinkable was the tragically inaccurate claim. My mother and I accompanied them.

I can't say I have clear memories of the Titanic, but some things have stayed with me forever. The panic. The pushing and shoving onto the lifeboats. The sound of screaming. The sound of the water lapping against bodies. The deafening silence as the screams stopped.

My mother and I had been separated from the rest of the family and as we stood on the side of the ship waiting for our rescue, she hastily clasped the Lincoln Penny around my neck and pushed a piece of paper explaining my history into my pocket. That was the last I saw of her or the rest of the family.

I was taken in by a thoroughly British and well-to-do family who had noble ideas of saving me. So now you know my dear. Posh old Aunt Josephine is only half-posh after-all. A scullery maid's daughter. You can imagine how much my parents wanted to keep that under wraps. They told me of course; it was their way of keeping me under control! Their way of making sure I towed the line. We mustn't let people know, just think of the shame...

How I have longed to kick against it all my life. Their snobbery and narrow mindedness drowned us all. I swore I wouldn't let this die with me but somehow the time never seemed right to tell you all. They trained me well you see.

But you, you are another generation entirely. You have freedoms that women of my time could only dream of. Take the penny (I believe they are worth quite a bit of money now), tell the world, don't tell the world, it is up to you. But most of all be happy in yourself.

I've known for a long time my darling, probably before you knew yourself. Please tell them. Living a lie is hell.

Yours affectionately,

Aunt Josie xx

I sat back, trying to take it all in. For now, it was the last paragraph that stood out the most. She'd known about me all along. And how funny that today of all days was the day I read this letter. After five years together, my parents would hear about my life partner for the first time. Tonight, I'd finally tell them about Lara.

Historical note–

The Lincoln cent or Lincoln penny as it is known was first struck in 1909 under Theodore Roosevelt. The designer was Victor David Brenner whose initials appear on the coins themselves. He was the first designer to have all his initials displayed in this way. His design was used on the penny until 1959. Today a 1909 Lincoln penny is worth around $117,500 or £90,000.

THE MUSEUM

The quaint little museum in the park had always fascinated me. Chock full of local artefacts and human-interest stories it was a magical little place. From the ancient wooden canoe to the tales of lifeboat disasters, I'd never grown tired of visiting.

Not all the rooms held the same appeal though. The room full of stuffed animals was one I normally avoided. And as for the one with all the dolls...ah yes, the dolls.

As ever, I found myself in there staring through the glass at row upon row of the exquisitely pretty, well dressed, well-coiffed play-things of privileged children. They repelled and attracted in equal measure. Their cold, intense, glass eyes seemed to follow the occupants of the room wherever they went. Those dead eyes seemed full of trapped souls silently screaming to get out. I shivered.

'We're closing in ten minutes,' said the lady who had welcomed me at the door with a fading leaflet.

'Thanks, I'll be along now,' I replied to her retreating back. I could hear her sensible shoes clacking down the sweeping staircase.

I'll never know what prompted me to do it, but suddenly I didn't want to leave. I was glued to the front of the display cabinet. Housing about a hundred dolls, it was the size of a small living room with floor to ceiling glass panels. Some dolls were artfully arranged in prams, some on chairs but many were simply lined up on shelves or on the floor. Tucked away at the far end of the cabinet was the doorway in.

Finding myself by this doorway, my fingers ran over the smooth glass seeking the handle. That too found its way into my hand and no one was more surprised than I to discover it was unlocked. I couldn't resist. Quickly checking I was alone, I turned the handle and the door opened.

I eased my way inside and picked a path through the dainty shoes and flouncy petticoats before crouching down by a huddle of rosy cheeked dolls. It was almost as if they were waiting for me. Looking more closely, their eyes all looked eerily the same. They shared the same haunted, stressed, intense stare as if they were trying to tell me something. I couldn't look away. Their dead irises drew me in like a magnet and I was drowning.

Gasping for breath, I felt trapped. I wanted to scream. To run flying from this place to the fresh air outside. Too late, the darkness came down as if I'd been hit.

* * *

The cabinet swam in front of my eyes before settling in a blurry haze. The darkness had gone but I still didn't feel right. My back felt stiff and locked in position. My arms felt heavy as lead and the effort of moving them was too much to contemplate.

Where was I?

As my eyes began to focus and take in my surroundings, I could see the woman from the front desk entering the viewing gallery.

I yelled frantically but my words had no effect on her. she didn't even glance my way. I stared at her, willing her to see me and come to my aid. I channelled all my remaining energy into that stare. Surely, she had to see me?

I watched as she slowly made her way around the room checking windows and locks. Wherever she went, my eyes followed her – boring into her neck, her back, her face, her eyes. I waited for a reaction, for recognition but none came.

Finally, she found herself by the display door. Bending over she picked up a discarded bag – my bag.

'Hello, anyone still here?' she called

Yes me! For the love of God, me! Get me out of here. Please help! Inside my head the words were ringing, piercingly loud but they had no effect on her.

'Is anyone still here?' she called again.

As the silence echoed and reverberated around the room, she shrugged her shoulders. Locking the cabinet door, she carried my bag away with her.

At the doorway she looked over her shoulder one last time. Looking straight at me, into my very being she simply said, 'Welcome to the collection.'

She turned out the light and left.

FINAL DESTINATION

Coddiwomple - an old English word meaning to travel purposefully towards a vague destination

I've always felt I've been travelling purposefully towards a vague destination. Everyone else seemed to have their lives sussed out. Their start and finishing point abundantly clear. Milestones for life laid down with particular care, each one pointing unwaveringly to the next.

Sometimes I envied them. Envied their easy, settled, secure lives. Envied the seeming ease with which they moved from child to teenager to adult to lover to career-maker to parent. Envied the way they knew what to say and what to wear for every occasion.

I was nothing like that. I'd always carved my own distinct path and nearly always in the face of opposition. My family didn't understand the cuckoo in their nest. I had four siblings who had fulfilled the expectations to perfection. Exam success, degrees, good jobs, suitable partners, 2.4 kids. It was all sickeningly wonderful.

Maybe, as the youngest, their perfection had set me off on my own journey of imperfection. The pressure to keep up leading me to create a very different life for myself.

Sure, I too had achieved exam success but then the fork in the road had appeared and I'd chosen the path that said, 'Destination Vague'.

I'll never forget announcing to my stunned family that I wouldn't be going to university. Nor would I be signing up for an apprenticeship or internship. Instead, I had plans to travel the world. Not for me the confines of this island, I wanted to see beyond the horizon.

'But what about University?' my distraught mother had asked.

'It's not for me. I have to deal with the wanderlust first.'

Sensing my parents' patent distress would follow me across the world I appeased them with a promise that I'd re-assess at the end of a year. They waved me off with the belief that I'd get it out of my system and then get my degree.

* * *

Nearly a year later, I'd sat on a remote beach in Western Australia. I'd been there for a few days and had decided to give some real thought to the promise I'd made to my parents. Stay or return?

I remember it all so vividly. It was nearly 5.00 pm and the sun although still hot had lost the fierce crackle that could sear through your flip flops (or thongs if you use the local lingo) in seconds. I sat in a little spot that I'd come to think of as mine and looked out to the pale turquoise sea. The gentle waves hid a beautiful world of colour just feet below the surface.

I picked up a handful of soft, pale, warm sand and let it trickle through my fingers. Scoop, trickle, scoop, trickle, scoop, trickle. As each tiny granule caressed my skin it seemed to hypnotise me. The tang of salt on my tongue, the smell of it in my nose, the feel of the sun on my skin, the sound of the birds and the colours that lit the landscape did their work. Thousands of miles from the happy home I'd grown up in, my urge to keep exploring the world had never been stronger. I was due to leave the next day, but it would be to continue the journey of my choice. There was no way I was going back!

* * *

That was forty years ago, and I never have looked back. Oh, I've returned from time to time – mostly to stock up on Marmite and proper tea bags. And the family have come to see me in the more sanitised places I've lived.

I've helped set up schools in ten different countries. I helped one community build a shower block, another a hospital and well. I've lazed on far flung beaches for weeks at a time, climbed mountains, crossed rivers and slashed my way through the jungle.

My travels have been full and never planned. Somehow the destinations decided themselves, however vague the idea was initially.

But now, after all these years, suddenly I do have a clear destination. It's certainly not one I chose. It, rather unfortunately, chose me.

'It's terminal,' the doctor had announced with the sympathetic bedside manner that years of medical training had perfected. 'There's nothing we can do other than keep you pain free.'

So, there we are, the final destination on this most glorious coddiwomple has been decided and NOT by me!

I can't say I'm thrilled or excited about the latest development in my travels. The butterflies in my tummy are doing a very different dance to normal. I may not have long but there are some things I have planned. Ironically, I've planned these final weeks with far more vigour and precision than any others in my life.

Yesterday, I arrived back at that remote beach in Western Australia. It has been my regular bolt hole over the years. I've almost become a local.

A couple of friends have constructed the most amazing open- fronted gazebo overlooking the sea. It's filled with a comfy bed, cushions and books with its very own ensuite Outback loo.

They have drawn up a strict rota to make sure I'm not alone when the final destination is reached. My siblings have also flown out to be here. We sit and reminisce about our childhood. Although we chose different paths, there is still a tie of affection that can't be broken.

Later today I'm speaking to a young man who has been busy making my final commission – my sea pod. Made from metal, the round container will house my ashes before being lowered to the seabed. There, I will lie amongst the colourful fish, the inquisitive crabs and the exotic corals. I'll lie there still as they start to settle on the metal surface, take hold and start to grow. The coral will strengthen, and the waters will be nourished.

My passing from this world will only mark another journey. Totally unknown, totally new and fresh. I will travel purposefully once more to another as yet very vague destination and if it's anything like this life, I will enjoy every second of it.

RACE FOR LIFE

The stalls are full of tense and nervous energy. We don't speak much. Sideways glances convey our emotions more effectively than words.

The hour is nearly upon us. All the months of training have been leading up to these frantic, terrifying minutes. Who knew how many of us would make it?

'Jed...Jed, can I ask you something?' The nervous voice of Donny pulled me back to the present.

'Sure Don, what's the problem?'

'What happens if I fall? Will Tucker help me up?'

I wasn't sure how to answer this. This was Donny's first season. The first time he'd been given the chance to take part. This could be his moment of glory. Should I tell him the truth or string him along?

I shook my hair back and contemplated whether a truth or a kind lie would be better. What would I have told my younger self?

'Look Don, don't think about that. Just keep your eye on the finish line. Head up, run like the wind and jump like your very existence depends on it.'

Well that last bit was definitely the truth if nothing else.

'Thanks Jed, I'll do that. Will it be much longer do you think? This waiting is killing me!'

'No, here comes Mr Hyland now and Tucker right behind. Look, best of luck and just think of the slap-up dinner we'll be enjoying in no time.'

There was no time for more. Mr Hyland was here to give me the final once over. His fingers would be digging in my ribs, feeling my legs, peering at my teeth. It was all so undignified.

Sighing, I stepped forward. I knew the drill. If Donny had hated the wait so far, this bit would be excruciating for him.

Prodding, poking, recording findings on a chart. Measurements taken, shoes checked. Accessories shiny, teeth gleaming, hair glossy. It was like being prepped for a catwalk show.

Finally, the moment was here. If I stretched my neck fully, I could just make out Donny. I tried to mouth one final 'good luck' but Mr Hyland was having none of it.

'Come on Jedemiah, it's time.'

Ugh, Jedemiah. I hated it when he called me that. The only thing worse was when he used my full name. Thankfully that didn't happen too often. I was much happier being plain old Jed.

But this of course, was not plain old Jed's moment. This wasn't even Jedemiah's, it was Mr Hyland's. As we walked toward the open track the anticipation and fear hit me afresh. The noise from the crowd enveloped us all. It was nerve wracking.

This was the absolute worst bit. The last couple of minutes before the race started was hell. Some runners would try to retreat, some would jostle and those of us who'd done this before, just waited. And at last everyone was ready. The call went out.

A hush went around the crowd, only the wind could be heard as it tickled our ears. Three, two, one...the race began.

I was off to a flying start using long even paces. I tore over the grass as if I had wings. I tried to ignore the incessant pain on my ribs and across my flank.

The first fence was coming. I could see Donny just ahead. He had a brilliant career ahead of him. He was so light and quick, and he landed with a gymnast's spring.

I touched down not far behind him. One down, fifteen to go.

My ears were ringing with the sound of the now rowdy crowds. No doubt all calling for their favourites. Not that we could hear any one name. Still it gave them something to do while we did the hard work.

Donny and I were neck and neck now. God he was a good runner - strong and sure. He was definitely on form today. I'd struggle to keep up at this pace.

Concentrate now Jed, another fence to negotiate. Damn it, that jarred. Never mind, keep going, don't think of it. Ignore the repeated whipping. Focus.

Another fence. Right, steady Jed, you can do it. That's better, much cleaner. Now find your stride. This is going well. Donny is still ahead but not by much. He's still in my reach. I can still do this...maybe.

The next fence, clean again. I'm starting to enjoy this. It's good to run the fidgets out of my legs. The whipping at my ribs has eased off too. I must be doing well. Mr Hyland will be pleased.

Donny is still going strong. I'm proud of him. He's done brilliantly for his first season. That boy is definitely one to watch. Deep down, I know I can't catch him. I wish him well; he really does deserve it. He's a nice lad too. Not bossy and snooty like some of the other runners I could mention.

Fence approaching, steady Jeddy, nice and easy. Cleared with inches to spare. We must be nearly halfway now. I'm starting to get tired and yes there's the return of the crop. I feel like I'm being used for drum practice!

Keep going Jed, ignore the pain, ignore the other runners. Look straight ahead. Fence coming. Clear!

On we go, that crop is really starting to bug me now. Despite what they think, it doesn't make us run any quicker. Ignore it, carry on, keep going. Donny is definitely pulling ahead. Come on Jed, time to add a bit of pace.

Ready for take-off, here we go – Wooaaaah, I wasn't expecting that! That should have been an easy jump. Where the hell did that grass come from and why is it over me instead of under me? Which way is up? And wow, that pain.

That's definitely not the crop. It's something else. God it hurts.

Right Jed, you know the score. Lie still, let the others pass you. Those thundering feet seem to be everywhere. No, they're going, off into the distance towards the finish line.

Well that's this race over for me. It was going so well. Next time, I'll do better next time. But oh, the pain, I've never known anything like this. I don't think I can move. My legs feel really strange, like they don't belong to me at all.

I think I'll just lie really still. The pain will pass in a minute. Mr Hyland will help. He'll know what to do. Yes, that's it, I'll just leave everything to Mr Hyland. He knows best. He'll look after me for sure. He won't let me be carted off like the others. He calls me his special boy; he'll make sure I get special treatment for definite.

And here he is. His face is looking a bit blurry and out of focus, but I can just make him out looking at me with some kind of horror. Blink Jed, look at him. Still blurry. And now it's raining. That's odd, the sky was cloudless when we set off. No, it's not rain, it's Mr Hyland. He is crouching next to me with tears streaming down his face. They are dripping from his chin and down onto my cheek. He stretches a hand and caresses my skin, gives one final pat then stands up. And just like that, I understand.

* * *

'Now for a round-up of today's sporting events. In the hotly anticipated Grand National there was an unexpected win for Hobson's Choice. The bookie's favourites Jedemiah Prince and Donny Be Good both fell. Unfortunately, both animals had to be destroyed.

'And finally, the football scores. Remember to look away if you don't want to see the results...'

MAGIC

The silky soft feathers ruffle in the wind. The strong, precise, yet ugly feet are poised to initiate flight. Muscles bunch under spreading wings and move in perfect harmony.

Under the moonlight the lake ripples and casts silver light into the greyest of places. The shadows are banished. The spotlight is ready to be filled.

The beating rhythm of wings and heart are the only things to break the silence of the night.

With utmost control, the wings dip, the shoulders prepare, the legs brace and with barely a splash he has landed. And now, all the strength and muscle is hidden in a glorious, sedate and ethereal glide. Pure grace in every delicate movement. His beauty shines in a manner to rival the moon.

This moment is his and his alone. He revels in it.

But not for long – the beating of many a wing banishes the solitude and serenity. The night is no longer his. He must fight to keep it for himself as one by one several more beautiful swans grace the surface of the lake.

He is ready for them. He is always ready for them. A dance that is beautifully sinister begins. Who will claim this territory? Who will have the moment? Who will be king?

Wings, beaks and shoulders all combine in strength and agility. Those long elegant necks become weapons of deadly stealth. The fight gathers pace and the ripples on the surface become jagged, harsh, broken and re-broken as wings fight for dominance. The momentum drags them in a writhing mass of feathers, legs and beady eyes from the water to dry land.

Here the fight continues. It should be ungainly, a series of inelegant waddles and comic pigeon toes. But even here the mastery of movement is a wonder to behold.

Wings and feather tips stretch and beguile. The flurry of movement at once fierce yet delicately formed. The battle goes on.

Beaks snap, eyes flash and necks bend and retract like snakes from ancient myths. Those strong, ugly feet beat a tattoo on the ground with accompanying hisses of fury.

Surely one swan cannot defeat all this alone. But it seems he can. for suddenly it is all over. The king retains his territory with an arrogant flick of his beak. The rest of the bevy back away, bow down, surrender. The moment is his once more.

The moonlight bathes the victor. He stands alone – tall, proud, composed. His arms poised above his head. His feet in perfect first position. His chest glistening with sweat.

Swan, or man? Man, or swan? The two so beautifully entwined even now they can't be sure.

Wild applause breaks the spell.

TIME

The box lay snug in my pocket wrapped up in a square of green silk.

I hastily tugged at the laces of my walking boots, making sure they were nice and secure before zipping up my coat. A warm, thick-knitted hat kept my short, springy, unruly hair tamed and my ears warm. Making sure the car was locked I turned and looked up.

There it was – the familiar rugged, foreboding cliff-like summit. 'The Tops' as we had always called it. I knew it was time.

Clouds were scudding across the sky in gusts and bursts. The odd white fluffy one trying desperately to be seen amongst the heavy grey and angry looking. The wind was rising – what she would have called a wuthering, withering day. The kind of day when the wind catches you unawares. One minute your friend pushing you along, the next turning on you and suffocating your mouth and nose.

But still, it was time.

The path was well trodden by hoof, paw and foot; the pathways clearly marked. My boots crunched on stones and dried droppings before negotiating a boggy puddle. She'd loved it here.

I'd found my walking stride now. Taking long, low, regular steps I covered the ground with surprising ease and speed.

Sucking in breaths of fresh air and raising my eyes to the waiting tops, I lumbered on.

I'd seen this place in every season and in every weather imaginable. This place was part of us just as we would become part of it.

It was time.

I slipped my hand into my pocket once more. Still there, still tied in the square of green silk.

Now for the challenging bit of the climb. The bit that left your legs wobbly, your chest aching, and your limbs exhausted. The bit that made you feel so incredibly alive!

Head down, arms swinging, legs striding, feet seeking foothold, fingers seeking bracken or rocks as an anchor.

And then – the reward! A panoramic view across the hills and valleys beyond. Birds swooping and diving, catching the wind beneath their feathers. The sun just glimpsing between the clouds.

I'd never tire of this place. We'd never tired of this place.

It was time.

Sitting down on the tuft that had become 'ours' over the years, I fished out the silk wrapped box. This was the first time it had been moved from the chest of drawers for five years.

Untying the green silk square, I snatched at it before the wind got to it and stuffed it deep into my pocket. It still retained her scent.

The box was beautiful. Hexagonal and small enough to fit in my palm, it was intricately carved. My fingers traced the patterns as they had once traced her skin.

It was time.

Heaving myself to my feet I lifted the box above my head and flipped up the lid.

Withering and wuthering the tiny dust particles swirled in the air and were gone.

TURQUOISE SARI

It caught her eye as the light touched it and seemed to make it live. Trailing from the corner of a cardboard box, the sari was the most beautiful thing Ann had ever seen. Turquoise shot through with silver and edged with a deep border of intricate patterns, it floated and danced its way up the path. The new neighbours were moving in.

Ann was both excited and nervous. Her previous neighbour Rosa had been a good friend. They'd spent many an hour righting the world or exchanging recipes over cups of tea and biscuits.

Rosa had finally moved out a month ago. She'd gone back to Barbados to enjoy the feel of the sun on a more regular basis than Britain could either promise or provide. She told Ann that she and Rob must visit but they both knew this would never happen. Since she'd gone, the house next door had been undergoing a lot of work. The kitchen and bathroom had been ripped out and decorators had been there bringing paint and wallpaper quite literally by the bucket load.

Ann watched with interest as the furniture and boxes were transported into Number 12. The furniture was elegant and expensive looking. Just like the couple following it down the path.

'Well that's that then. They won't want to hang around with us,' said Ann turning away from the window.

'What's that?' Rob lifted his head from the newspaper.

'The new neighbours. They look so elegant and sophisticated. They look, I dunno, interesting. I can't see me popping 'round for a cuppa and cosy chat.' Ann tried not to sound bitter.

'Remember when we first moved in and Rosa came 'round to welcome us with her ginger cake? You two became thick as thieves even though she was much older than you. You might just be surprised.'

Ann looked at Rob and smiled. 'You're right, I'll dig Rosa's recipe out now.'

* * *

Carrying the ginger cake carefully in layers of grease proof paper, Ann knocked hesitantly on the door. The woman who opened it looked friendly, if a little distracted. Her long dark hair, almond shaped eyes and cheek bones a model would pay good money for all contributed to her beauty. Ann felt her heart sink a little.

'Sorry to disturb you. I'm Ann from next door, Number 14. I just thought I'd welcome you to the street. I've made ginger cake.' She was babbling. She just knew she was going to do that.

A beautiful smile lit up the woman's face as she took the cake from Ann. 'Thanks, that's so kind. I'm Anjali.'

'Well, when you've unpacked, you must come 'round for a cup of tea.'

'We'd love that. Here's my husband. Kavindu, this is Ann, Ann – Kavindu although most of the time we just call him Kav.'

'Nice to meet you Ann,' said Kav as he shook hands heartily. Not strictly good looking but with a smile that transformed his face, Kav looked genuinely pleased to meet her.

'We're having a few friends 'round next Saturday, why don't you and your husband, partner...'

'Er husband, he's my husband. His name's Rob.'

'Great, well why don't you and Rob come?' Kav enthused.

'Lovely. Er look, I'll leave you to unpack. I know you must be up to your eyes.'

Ann scuttled back down the path and into her own house. As she shut the front door she felt like weeping. They were everything she'd once known. Glamorous, confident and fun. And above all, interesting. Even their names were interesting. I mean honestly Rob and Ann: one syllable of ordinariness. Whereas Anjali and Kavindu sounded like poetry. Their friends were bound to be glamorous too. She and Rob would stick out like a sore thumb and a dull one at that!

* * *

Two days later Anjali knocked on the door.

'I'm off work this week, so I took a chance that you'd be in. I wasn't sure if you'd be working.'

Ann led Anjali through to the sitting room which screamed: KIDS LIVE HERE!

'Me, er no, not at the moment. I'm looking after the kids. Archie is four, he's at school and Isla is two. She's just having her nap.'

'We haven't got around to having kids yet despite the prospective grandparents' encouragement.' Anjali laughed with a touch of tension.

'So, what do you do?' Ann asked hurriedly to cover the moment of awkwardness.

'Oh, I'm in media. Assistant producer for a daytime show based in Media City. That's why we've moved really. It's a bit shorter commute from this end of town. Kav's a GP and his practice is over this way anyway. It made sense to move.'

Ann could have guessed; even their jobs were important or dynamic. The most dynamic thing she did these days was get Archie to school on time and unload the dishwasher one-handed while Isla clung to her like a monkey. Despite the slight feeling of discontent, Ann couldn't help but like Anjali. She had a ready laugh and was easy to talk to. Ann started to relax and by the time two cups of tea and the inevitable piece of cake had been consumed, a friendship was starting to blossom.

'Don't forget the gathering next Saturday. Bring the kids, it's going to be a lot of fun. We'll have Bhangra too.'

'What's Bhangra? Is it like Bollywood?' asked Ann nervously.

'Kind of. It's Indian disco dancing for want of a better way to describe it. You'll love it. We do this every couple of months. The saris come out and sometimes we put Mendhi on our hands. That's the beautiful orange brown patterns you sometimes see on Asian women's hands. We can paint yours too. If you like.'

Once Ann would have thrilled at the thought of Mendhi and Bhangra. She'd loved trying new things, finding inspiration and letting her imagination run away with her – once. As Anjali made her way out, Ann felt slightly sick. The hand-painting she could cope with but dancing? The only dancing she did these days was to the latest inane children's jingle. Dancing in front of adults, the thought terrified her. And Rob's reaction wasn't much better when she told him of the treat in store for them.

'Dancing!' he exclaimed, nearly choking. 'I'm not dancing for anyone. Are you sure you want to go?'

'We'll have to, or it will look rude. We'll go for half an hour. We won't be able to stay long anyway. I'll have to bed the kids down.'

'Well I'm not dancing – I'm telling you that for nothing.'

The next day, Ann got on with the drudgery of day-to-day life. The never-ending washing, ironing, cooking, cleaning. It seemed to suck all the joy out of her. But then she'd catch a glimpse of Isla sucking the very tip of her thumb while she slept. Or, Archie would bring home a drawing just for her and the joy flooded back in.

On Tuesday as she was putting some of Archie's toys away in his bedroom, she spotted Anjali hanging out her washing. No plain old socks, pants and t-shirts for her but a raft of beautiful, exquisite saris. A rainbow filled her washing line and the sun reflected off the silver and gold thread and the tiny mirror pieces.

There was the turquoise one she'd spotted the other day. Ann couldn't help but stare at it. It seemed to embody everything she wanted to be – vibrant, alive and glamorous. She imagined how it would feel to wear it and the confidence a simple piece of material would give her. The colour would set off her skin perfectly. She wondered if Anjali would let her try it on. Woah! Stalker territory. You can't just ask to wear someone's clothes when you've only just met them. Ann closed the toy chest on that idea quickly and picked her way through the Lego minefield to the door.

As for what she'd wear on Saturday? She hadn't got a clue. There was absolutely nothing in her wardrobe that could compete with the saris and colours that would be on display. She'd probably have to opt for the safe option, jeans and a top. How had she become so dull and boring?

* * *

On Thursday, Ann opened the front door to find Anjali there with a bulging bag of material.

'Do you have five minutes to spare?'

'Yes of course, come in. 'Scuse the mess. The kids leave stuff everywhere; I'm always tidying up but never seem to get on top of it.' She was babbling again.

'Ann, seriously, don't worry about it. Look, I hope you don't mind me asking this and you can say no if you don't want to, but I just wondered if you wanted to wear one of my saris on Saturday? Everyone else will be wearing one so it might make you feel a bit more included. What do you think? I won't be at all offended if you say no, honestly.' For once, Anjali was babbling too.

'I brought some to pick from just in case.' She upended the bag and a flood of colour gushed over the neutral carpet and across the rug. Instantly the room felt a little bit more alive.

'I would love to!' enthused Ann. With a gasp she dived into the silks letting them pour through her fingers and over her arms and legs. There were so many to choose from and all so exquisite. At the bottom was the one she sought – the turquoise sari. With trembling fingers, she pulled it gently from the pile and held it up against herself. A memory from another life tugged at her.

'Could I wear this one?'

'Of course, it will really suit you.'

As Anjali showed Ann how to drape herself in the folds of material Ann felt a change come over herself. She felt elegant and dainty. She'd become more assured and confident. She actually felt beautiful. But most of all she felt interesting. Interesting to know and interesting to be with. She swirled and twirled around her dull little sitting room and felt as if she were in a palace.

'Ann you look like a different person. Look at you, you are stunning!' Anjali hugged her spontaneously and Ann felt the germ of an idea start inside her.

While Anjali quickly changed into a dark green sari which made her skin glow radiantly, Ann allowed the idea to play in her mind. The women sat down in their silken splendour to enjoy tea and biscuits.

'You know, before I had the kids, I was a clothes designer and maker. It's how Rob and I met actually. He came to fit out the shop I rented a workspace in. Quirky but wearable clothes, that was the idea. It seemed to work. People liked the clothes and I was starting to get a name for myself, just locally but I loved it.'

'So why did you stop?'

'Oh because of the kids. It was my choice; Rob was happy for me to carry on, but I wanted to be with them. I gave up the workshop and the only sewing I've done since Archie came along is for them.'

'Have you any of your old pieces here? I'd love to see them,' asked Anjali genuinely interested.

Ann's stomach lurched. She hadn't shown anyone her work for such a long time. But maybe it was time to be brave and bold again. 'Er, OK, give me a minute.'

Ann gathered up her turquoise skirts and ran lightly up the stairs into Isla's bedroom. Creeping past the sleeping toddler she opened the wardrobe and extracted the three remaining signature designs she had kept. An elegant work dress with side pockets, a vibrant blouse with Chinese style piping around the cuffs and collar and a baggy jumpsuit that looked almost like a long dress. These had been really popular.

Tiptoeing back past Isla she ran down the stairs and gave the pieces to Anjali.

She sat down biting her nails. What if she hated them or thought they were rubbish? Ann closed her eyes in anguish. Anjali picked the pieces up and slowly turned them this way and that. She stood up and held the work dress up against herself.

'I love this! Would you be able to make me one?'

'Of course, I've got an idea for the material too.'

'How much would it be?'

'Look, I'm happy to make one but I don't want you to pay me. Honestly, it's fine. It's been so long since I did anything like this, I wouldn't want to charge you for it just in case.'

'No, no, I insist. If you won't take any money, I won't order.'

The idea that Ann had been playing with suddenly seemed like a real possibility.

'I don't want payment Anjali, but you could help me with something else. Your saris have given me an idea. Could you source some that people don't want anymore? I'd like to up-cycle them into my range. I'd make the same signature pieces plus skirts and sleeveless tops using the sari material. I was thinking I'd do your dress the same way. What do you think? Do you think people would like them?'

'Like them, I think they'd LOVE them. It's a great idea. As for saris, leave it to me, I can ask the girls to bring a couple each on Saturday.'

Ann's eyes shone with anticipation. This is what she'd been missing. She'd allowed the interesting, creative Ann to be swallowed up and she was the only one who could bring her back. She'd have her own interest and business again, something to think about other than washing, shopping and cooking. Rob would be supportive; he'd always said he was happy for her to carry on designing. She'd be herself again.

What to call the business? She wanted a new name to signify the new start. Sari-cycle? Splash of Colour? Silk Cuts? Nothing was really singing to her. But then it struck her. Of course, the name had been staring at her all the time. Turquoise Sari.

And right there in the middle of her cluttered, child-centred room Ann's re-incarnation began.

THE ROCK POOL

The sea has always sung its own song just for me. An orchestra of sounds from soft and gentle to a crescendo of thundering roars. It pulls me in like the sirens of old. I want to touch it, feel it, immerse my whole self in it. I want to be one of the waves which dance up the beach tickling children's toes.

A seagull calls and I turn my eyes from the water. There it goes inland towards the easy pickings of scratchings and chips. A minor distraction, no more. My eye returns to the water. The tide will be turning soon. The symphony is about to begin, and I don't want to miss a note.

'Excuse me,' a rich, deep voice startles me. 'I was just wondering if this was yours?'

I glance up and my breath catches slightly. I've never believed in all that nonsense about love at first sight – not until now. No doubt you are waiting for a description of this paragon, but I have none. All I know is he has the kindest eyes I've ever seen. Unusual, dark stormy grey, full of humour and the longest lashes imaginable. His skin is like looking at pale chocolate. He's a smiler. I can tell from the slight crinkles at the edge of each beautiful eye. He smiles now.

'Sorry, I didn't mean to startle you. I just wondered if this was yours?'

He is holding out his hand and cupped in the palm is a bracelet. A silver bracelet hung with just three silver charms, a shell, a harp and a paintbrush.

'No, it's not mine,' I manage to croak.

How pathetic and ungainly my voice sounds next to his smooth baritone. A beautiful voice for radio as my mother would have put it. Pulling myself together I look at him again and attempt further, less dreary conversation.

'Where did you find it?'

'Just over there, by the rock pool.' He points off to the right.

I know exactly where he means. I know and have captured every inch of this beach. It's practically part of me.

We turn without words and walk towards the pool encased by rocks. Unusually for me, he's a little bit taller than I am and his magnificent Afro is nearly close enough to tickle my cheek. My long, straggly blonde hair tries to entangle it in the wind. I hastily pull it together in my hand and tuck it down the back of my top. As we walk, I scour the beach –deserted – it often is. Exactly the reason I like it here. Together, we clamber up to the edge of the pool. There is a rough collection of rocks which serve as a seat. I lean down from my craggy cushion, remove my flip-flops and place them on the side. I dip my toes into the water. It's chilly but not unbearable.

'I'm Winston by the way.'

'Nice to meet you Winston, I'm Karen.'

This so-called ice breaker does the exact opposite and silence descends. Luckily the sound of the ocean fills the gap. As each wave rushes in it returns to the sea with a little bit of awkwardness until there's just Winston and Karen sitting by the side of the rock pool content to know one another.

I realise I'm still clutching the bracelet and I turn each charm over in my hands.

'I wonder what these charms mean to whomever this belongs to? It's funny really because they could have been made for me.'

'Why's that then?' invites Winston.

'Well, the shell for starters. The beach is my place. I come here every day. It's part of me and I'm part of it. It's where I'm me.' I stop abruptly, embarrassed about what I'm revealing. Winston will surely think I'm odd at best or unhinged at worst. Either that or some beach dwelling hippie who spends her day looking for auras. The hippie bit isn't that far off although my search is for something other than colourful auras.

'I know what you mean.' He surprises me. 'I feel as if everywhere else is just somewhere I exist or pass through. Here though, I'm Winston. This is somewhere that accepts me unconditionally.'

We exchange glances until I break the look and fumble once more for the charms.

'As for the harp, the sea and music are one and the same thing to me. The sea makes music, the music fills the sea. I think it's my most favourite sound in the world. I'll never tire of it, it's never dull and it's beautiful. I like to think of it as my own perfect orchestra.' I'm gushing again.

We both gaze out to the horizon. The songs of the spray and the birds wash in with the tide.

'I've never thought of it like that before but you're right.' Winston's voice adds to the melody being carried towards us. 'It's like listening to the most harmonious, perfect piece of music in the world.'

Even the breeze is joining in and stirs little ripples around my toes. I lift my feet out and dry them on the edge of my tie dye skirt which I then wrap around my knees and legs. I rest my chin on top of my knees and continue to gaze at the sea.

'And the paintbrush?' asks Winston.

'Ah the paintbrush. Well, I suppose you could say the brush is what brings me here. It's the reason I spend every day down here.' I stop and glance at Winston. 'I'll explain another day.' I'm not ready to give away everything about myself just yet.

'I was wondering if you'd give me the opportunity to ask and now you have. Would you maybe like to meet me tomorrow? I could bring a picnic and we could listen to the sea and maybe you could tell me about the paintbrush?'

'It would be easier to show you,' I laugh. 'I'd like that Winston, I'd like that very much. And now, I'll have to go. I'll see you tomorrow about noon?'

'I look forward to it Karen.' He lifts his hand by way of goodbye as I negotiate my way down the rocks.

With a final glance over my shoulder and quick wave I run back up the beach. The sound of the ocean follows me as it always does. But this time, it sings a song I've never heard before...

'Er, excuse me madam.'

This voice is neither deep nor rich and it jars through my very being. Turning I look, not into the eyes of my beloved Winston but the eyes of a stranger. A kindly looking face but a stranger, nonetheless.

'I'm very sorry madam but we close in ten minutes. Could you start to make your way out?'

Stifling a sigh, I pick up my handbag, the silver charms on my wrist dancing along the metal clasp until the shell catches as it always does. Disentangling the charm for what must have been the millionth time since Winston found it, I glance back up at the painting on the wall.

The painting I'd been vowing to track down ever since we sold it all those years ago. I knew as soon as the buyer left our cottage, I'd made a mistake and so did Winston. For this was the only one of my seascapes to feature people. The images were small, but immaculately, I'd recreated Winston and me on our rocky seat gazing out to the orchestra in the sea.

Oh, the cruel irony that the painting should be found just as my Winston had been lost. Tumbled through the stormy waters of illness and dragged back out with the riptide of grief.

Forcing my eyes, my heart and my very being from the painting, I had one final mission. Smiling to the young man who had brought me back to the present with such a crash I allowed the shiny lights of the gift shop to pull me in. For once, it suited my purpose perfectly.

Passing the glossy re-print and money to the girl behind the counter I became aware of her words.

'Beautiful painting isn't it? We were lucky to get it in our collection. Karen Fountain never normally put people in her work. It's so rare. Are you a fan?'

'In a way,' I said.

Smiling sadly, I turned and made my way to the door with Winston clutched in my hand.

THE NATIVITY

A small boy with a permanently snotty nose stands barefoot with a tea towel on his head.

The rehearsals seem to have lasted his lifetime. The safe sanctuary of school has been changed into a chaotic mass of costumes and concert songs on a loop.

The teachers and staff have veered from controlled to teary to barely contained hysteria and back again. The whole process has been like herding cats.

Sonny knows a lot about cats. His nan has four. He loves to feel their soft fur under his sticky fingers. They don't shout at him for being in the way. Nor do they forget he's even in the room.

Sonny wishes they were here to see his moment. Sonny has a part, a speaking part. One line but oh so important

'There's a stable 'round the back.'

Wiping his dripping nose on his 'rustic' tunic he steps onto the stage. His eyes scan the crowd hungrily searching for the one person who won't forget to come. The hall is crowded with parents, grandparents and small children who have been bribed with bottles, dummies and snacks to keep them quiet.

He stretches on tiptoe and there she is. Right at the back clutching a hankie to her own dripping nose. 'Happy tears,' thinks Sonny.

She looks right at him and blows a kiss. Smiling, Sonny steps forward and delivers his small but important line.

And at the back of the room Nan's face wrinkles into a smile of pride and love.

THE SPACE IN OUR DAYS

The space in our days is full of people we don't see anymore. Those childhood friends who helped you climb trees, make dens or make the best mud pies in town.

Or the teenage support network who held your hand and dried your eyes, as yet another rat bag broke your heart.

And the University 'best friends for life' who have drifted from regular meet ups to letters, then Christmas cards and now, inevitably to the birthday messages prompted by Facebook.

The spaces they leave are filled with others who define their own roles in your life.

The spaces that truly can't be filled are the ones left by the dearly departed – the irreplaceable ones. The parents who are taken too soon. Their spaces at Christmas, family gatherings, weddings, Christenings and even funerals are never truly filled. Others may come close, spreading their own unique glow but it will never burn as brightly as the original.

That space will only ever be theirs and it fills our days with nostalgic reminders, tears and laughter.

The space in our days is full of memories.

WOODLOT

The tree house community had been there for hundreds of years. Long before the term 'tree house' was even used. Back then (and even to this day), it was simply known as Woodlot to those who lived there. And to those who didn't live there? Well, first you have to be aware that something exists before you can give it a name.

The community had lived in peace and harmony for many years. They'd adapted with the times and from the initial basic platforms, Woodlot was now a rich tapestry of homes that George Clarke would be proud of.

A complicated system of pulleys, rope ladders and bridges linked the trees and their dwellers around a centrally cleared area where the communal fire was never allowed to go out.

The trees were all strong and sturdy oaks. Their spread eagle branches the perfect support system for houses amongst the leaves. The oaks were not the only trees used in the making of the homes though. The evergreens were lopped down to form a watertight roof cover and beech trees had been hewn and planed to make the floors and sides. And as the family numbers had multiplied some of these houses now had multiple layers – the original high rises minus the concrete. The scent of wood, green and growth mingled with the individual smells of the occupants to create a heady perfume.

One dwelling was full of more scents than others – it

belonged to Alvina. Lower down than everyone else's it was accessible by a gentle slope rather than the usual rope ladder.

At the top of the slope was a shrine full of flowers, pebbles, pinecones and other lovingly chosen gifts and offerings. Once you ducked down under the low hanging herbs at the door you straightened up into a surprisingly cavernous room. A brightly coloured curtain divided the space. No one had ever seen behind it.

In the centre of the room a fire flickered. A very small affair contained inside a metal bowl where the wood glowed brightly. A frame had been built over this fire to hang cooking pots from. Some days the smells from this pot were almost overpowering, some days they appeared to be nothing more exciting than water.

The walls contained shelf after shelf of labelled jars – all in alphabetical order. All at just the right height without having to stretch uncomfortably or squint too hard. Around the edge of the space were benches strewn with cushions and blankets in comforting earthy colours. There was a distinct air of healing, well-being and calm.

I've never forgotten the first time I went in...

* * *

I didn't grow up in Woodlot, I was an outsider. My beginnings were very different. Born fifty miles away in a bustling commuter town I led a very conventional life until I was 18. Nice family, nice school, nice friends. Everything was so nice and well-ordered that it didn't occur to me to question if it was what I wanted from life.

The summer I finished my A levels was a pivotal moment. My mates, Phil, Jeff and I had packed a tent, basic supplies and booze (obviously) and headed to the 'country' for a camping trip. Phil had designated himself chief organiser and had used an OS map to select a suitable spot.

'There's a thick wooded area here, looks about an hour's walk from Bescar Brae train station. I reckon that will do us.'

And that was that. Planning over, mission decided, destination confirmed. Anticipation is an intoxicating feeling and coupled together with youth, optimism and cider, it was at fever pitch.

We left the station and with Phil at the front, headed for our wooded campsite for the night.

'Has anyone actually been camping before?' Jeff asked as we traipsed up the road.

'Once with Scouts, it was a bit of a disaster. It chucked it down all weekend and the tent I was in was leaking. I vowed never again, but here I am!' I said adjusting my rucksack more comfortably. 'How about you Phil?'

'Yeah we used to go a lot when I was a kid. My folks thought it was important we learnt how to make fires, sleep outside, that kind of stuff. Character-building they called it.'

'Well I've never been. I'm starting to think it might not actually be for me.' Jeff had a tendency to whinge and Phil and I exchanged glances that spoke volumes.

'You'll be fine!' I assured him. 'Campfire, cider, sausages and marshmallows. And Phil will get us through it.'

'All right Dan, but I hold you responsible if I come home bitten alive and hungover.'

We all laughed. Jeff's inability to hold any kind of alcohol was legendry.

We'd left the road system a mile or so back and had been skirting fields and meadows for some time. Eventually, the woods had appeared on the horizon and now, in front of us, a path that would take us directly to the entrance was just a few hundred feet away. The trees swayed gently in the summer breeze, a montage of every shade of green imaginable. The leaves seem to be whispering to us, beckoning us in.

As we entered the woods, the canopy of leaves hid the sun and the sounds from the outside world. All we could hear were the animals in the undergrowth, birds in the trees and of course Jeff's whining.

'Seriously though lads, won't we get eaten alive in here?' he queried with a look of panic in his eyes.

'Once the fire's going, the bugs will stay away. Stop worrying. This is going to be fun,' insisted Phil. 'First things first, let's get the fire set up.' Phil dumped his rucksack in a clearing we'd found deep in the woods. 'Let's go three ways and gather as many sticks, twigs and small logs as possible. See you back here in ten.'

Knowing my own ability at getting lost, I stayed long enough to knot my old school tie to a branch as a marker before joining the hunt. A quick look over my shoulder gave me a glimpse of Jeff swatting at the air around his head before cautiously setting off in another direction. I wasn't sure he'd last the weekend.

As I scoured the ground for suitable firewood, I gave my mind over to thoughts of the future. I had a place at University providing my results were up to it but now the time was getting closer I wasn't sure that Economics was for me. It was all so dull and sensible. I was done with sensible. I wanted to do something that mattered. Something with a real purpose – anything but bloody Economics!

My arms were getting full of fuel when the scream and the bite of metal on metal split the air. Dropping the wood, I turned towards the sound.

'Help! Dan! Jeff! It's my bloody foot, it's in a trap!' Phil's voice sounded anguished and I set off at a run.

Stumbling through the undergrowth I found Phil who was white- faced and practically passed out. His left foot was held in the iron teeth of a savage animal trap. The blood oozed down the fangs over his shoe and onto the ground where it was pooling under his ankle. I swallowed my nausea and took a step forward.

Funnily enough my nice school hadn't prepared me for what to do if your friend gets caught in a trap and I was woefully ill-prepared. Steadying my breath, I touched the trap gently. Obviously not that gently as Phil let out a howl of pain. Thankfully Jeff arrived at that point. I say thankfully as if I expected him to have acquired the skills of a surgeon in the ten minutes since I'd seen him. Jeff took one look at Phil's foot and promptly vomited in the bushes. Great.

'Right, we need to slow the bleeding. We'll have to raise the foot trap and all,' I said with a calm I was far from feeling.

Jeff wiped his mouth, looked at Phil's face and whispered, 'Won't it hurt him?'

Containing my irritation, I gave a curt nod but simply said,

'We'll have to do it Jeff.'

Glancing around, I noticed what looked like some kind of official log pile. A solitary log lay off to the side and we rolled it over to act as a prop. I knelt down by Phil and told him our plan.

'On three, we're going to lift your foot and prop it on the log to stop the bleeding. Then I'm going to go for help and leave Jeff here. Ok?'

Phil nodded weakly. Frankly, I don't think he cared what we did at that point.

Anyone who has ever had to knowingly inflict pain on another human, even if it's for their own good will tell you that the last second before you act is the worst. Jeff and I looked at each other, laid a hand each on leg and trap and with a deep breath lifted it as one. It was so heavy I didn't think we'd be able to hold it but somehow, we did. As we lowered it onto the log Phil gave a whimper and mercifully passed out from pain.

'Jeff, stay here with him. Check his pulse regularly, keep him warm. I'll be back as soon as I can.' Staying only to strip off my shirt and throw it at Jeff I turned on my heel and ran.

* * *

Crashing my way through the undergrowth and dodging the trees I ran until my sides ached. Scanning left and right for the path to take me back towards the entrance to the woods, I realised I'd set off blindly with no clue as to where I was going. Cursing myself for my stupidity I forced myself to stop and think.

I bent over and drew in deep gulps of air. As my breathing returned to normal, I became aware of an odd sensation. I could have sworn something – or someone – was watching me. Glancing warily around I called out nervously: 'Hello! Anyone there? I need help.'

The last thing I expected was a response so when it came, I jumped out of my skin. Right in front of my startled eyes, the bush parted and out stepped the most beautiful creature I'd ever seen. Before you start worrying about my state of mind, I don't mean a mythical creature, I mean a young woman maybe three or four years older than me who was very real and very human.

She had long dark hair which plunged down her back in a tumbled coil of curls and waves. Her fringe was a stark contrast of silver grey which curved down below her chin. Tucking the silver hair behind her ear she looked at me with eyes that were the most glorious blue/violet I'd ever seen. Her nose had an alluring crookedness and her lips hinted at a smile.

'You said you needed help? What's the matter?' Her voice was deep and husky. It captured me where I stood.

Pulling myself together I brought my thoughts back to Phil and Jeff. God Phil, he could literally be dying as I stood there.

'Yes, it's my friend. He's caught his foot in a trap, there's blood everywhere. I've left my other friend with him but Phil's bleeding. Badly. I don't know what to do but he definitely needs an ambulance. He's over by a log pile that way,' I pointed a shaking hand.

'Come with me first. My medicines aren't far.' And with that she turned on her heel and ran.

I followed her through the trees until we arrived at the settlement of houses in the trees. The beauty of the community didn't strike me then. My thoughts were too full of Phil and what might happen. Pausing only to smile briefly at a man and woman tending the fire I reached the open doorway the woman had disappeared through.

Stepping inside was like entering another world. I was immediately filled with an overwhelming sense of calm and peace. The smells of the herbs mingled with the wood and I inhaled it all. I sank gratefully into the cushions.

'I'm Alvina by the way. Just give me a minute to gather what I need.' She darted along the shelf opening jars and retrieving various plants and herbs. She flung them into a small cauldron like pot and then moved to a small gong outside her front door. The sound it produced echoed around the settlement and out into the trees beyond. It was deafening but effective.

The two people at the fire were quickly joined by men,

women and children of all ages. Between them they had an old wooden door, ropes, blankets and what looked like a container of water.

'This man's friend needs our help. He's by the log pile with an animal trap wound to his foot, in need of urgent medical attention. Let's go.' As one, the people followed Alvina and I back through the woods.

'So why are you and your friends here?' She passed quickly over the woodland floor and seemed scarcely out of breath despite the rapid pace.

'We're camping for the weekend. It was supposed to be a bit of fun after our exams. We've just finished at Sixth Form in Wroxchester,' I answered breathily.

'How did you find out about the woods? Not many people come here for the day never mind for camping. We like it that way.'

'Phil saw it on an OS map. He thought it looked nice. We didn't know it was private. Sorry.' I was getting a stitch again.

'It's not private, we just don't often see people here which is why it's perfect for our community. Welcome to Woodlot by the way.' Alvina held a branch back as we passed through yet more undergrowth. She obviously knew the woods like the back of her hand, unlike me. After what seemed like forever, we came to a bit that looked vaguely familiar. My school tie was flapping in the wind like a pathetic talisman. Not far to go now.

'Phil! Jeff! We're coming!' I yelled.

And then the woods seemed full of activity. The Woodlotters streamed past me and set to rescuing Phil, who had regained consciousness. A fire was made for Alvina's pot and her herbs were thrown into the soon bubbling water.

While the water boiled, two of the women had gently moved Jeff out of the way before another stuck a long piece of metal into the mechanism of the trap around Phil's foot and somehow released the jaws. They sprung apart with a sickening clunk. At that point Alvina appeared with a cloth and a mug. Giving the mug to one of the women she watched as Phil gulped the contents before relaxing into a gentle sleep.

As soon as his eyes closed, she set about removing Phil's

mangled shoe. I shuddered when I looked at it. It would be a miracle if he could walk again. With the shoe out of the way, Alvina and a young man cleaned the wound. When Alvina selected a needle and some kind of twine to stitch the wound, I took myself off to sit with Jeff. Economics might not be my career of choice anymore, but medicine was definitely off the list too.

Phil was lifted gently onto the old door, smothered in blankets and secured with ropes. The Woodlotters had insisted we all return to the camp with them. Jeff was in no state to pitch a tent and I was weary beyond belief, so we'd accepted gratefully.

'Tomorrow we'll send Phil to the nearest hospital in the Land Rover. Taryn will take him,' Alvina announced as she invited Jeff and I into her dwelling.

Jeff seemed to have recovered somewhat and was looking curiously around the room. His eyes got wider as he took it all in.

'Shouldn't he go tonight though?' As efficient as Alvina was, I didn't want Phil getting gangrene or tetanus.

'Believe me, the best thing he can get right now is rest. He'll be watched all night. Funnily enough we make studying medicine and healing a priority out here.'

'Of course, I didn't mean to imply you didn't know what you were doing!' I could barely apply a plaster never mind repair a man's foot so who was I to question?

Alvina smiled tightly and ladled some kind of broth into bowls for Jeff and me to eat. I'm not sure how long we sat in that room, but everything imprinted itself on my senses; the taste of the broth, the scent of the wood, the feel of the cushions, the sight of all those herbs in the jars and the comforting sound of bubbling water. I didn't want to leave. Not ever.

And I suppose in a way I haven't. Sure, we got Phil off to hospital the next day and thankfully he was OK apart from a limp and a dramatic scar which he still likes to show off to unsuspecting strangers, but I never did take up that place to study Economics. Instead, I spent the rest of that summer at Woodlot. The woods and its people had saved Phil and now I wanted to do something in return. I wanted to preserve and care for the trees for future generations. When I should have been packing my bags for Uni, I was starting an apprenticeship as a Tree Surgeon. The college was great, but the true learning was done with the best in the business – Jacob and Mal in Woodlot. They taught me how to listen to the trees, how to feel their pain but most importantly, how to encourage re-growth and sustainability.

After three years under their watchful eye they deemed me experienced enough to be let loose on the general public's trees and woodland. I'd found a job that was both useful and needed. Even better, they'd accepted me into their community. I was one of them.

Now each night when I return to my own dwelling in the settlement, I reflect on how lucky I was to meet Alvina. She has delivered babies into our community (including mine), saved lives, eased pains and given comfort when needed. We've all felt those cushions beneath us in times of trouble. We've all supped from her cauldron of hope. Every community needs a heart and Alvina's home was ours.

Like all mere mortals, Alivina can't live forever but she is prepared for this too. Just last week she called a meeting around the central fire to announce who her own apprentices would be. My wife and I felt tears prickle as Meridi, our daughter's name was announced. For the next five years she and her husband Finn will devote themselves to Alvina and her teachings. The future of Woodlot is secure.

.

UNTIDY SHOES

The view from the window was glorious! A wide expanse of meadow which had been exquisitely decorated with poppies, cornflowers and other wildflowers sloped away towards the cliff edge. Beyond it lay the sea. The Atlantic Ocean caressed and smashed the rocks and pebbles on the beach which lay out of sight.

Douglas was unmoved by the idyllic view before him. His mind was frantically turning phrases and words over. A spark of an idea quickly extinguished by crushing self-doubt. He was getting nowhere.

The week away had been Fletcher's idea.

'Take yourself off. Get the damn thing written and then we can talk about us.'

'Talk about us.' If ever a statement was designed to give birth to dread, that was surely it. Douglas hadn't even noticed. But he had leapt at the chance of a week away to focus on his latest book. He'd arrived the night before as the final beams of sun had been calling the night out to play.

A city dweller by nature, Douglas hadn't taken in his surroundings as he'd unpacked the car, located the corkscrew and released a gush of red into a large glass. He'd flung his jacket on the couch, eased his tatty Converse shoes off his feet, yawned and settled into a large, comfortable chair.

He'd dig his writing gear out in the morning. For now, he was going to relish being in a nag-free zone. He took a generous mouthful of wine. Fletcher meant well but he had no idea how the creative mind worked. It didn't fit into his neat, tidy, OCD world. It was messy, packed, busy and unpredictable. Sometimes it forgot the real world as the fictional one took over. How could one be expected to remember mundane activities like buying bread, putting on the dishwasher or cooking dinner when the imaginary world of Jack Mackerel had hold? Unfortunately, Fletcher expected exactly that.

'You spend more time with that Jack Mackerel than you do with me!' The accusation had been flung at him on more than one occasion. Fletcher was right though. Jack had become part of Douglas' life and was as real to him as some of his friends and family. More so in some cases.

Douglas swirled the remaining wine around the glass before emptying it in a gulp. Leaving his shoes untidily on the floor (this was definitely not allowed at home) he took himself off to bed.

* * *

The gulls woke him early. Their screeching burrowed into his brain and banished sleep. He retrieved his phone from the bed side table – 6.14 am. He groaned and was about to put it down again when the message symbol caught his eye. He tapped it with his thumb.

'Presume you arrived safely. Hope it's productive for you. F x.'

Why did Fletcher always make him feel so damned guilty? Ok, so he hadn't texted. He should have done but he didn't. Fletcher should know what he was like by now. A small nagging voice from deep inside his conscience made itself heard. 'He'd have texted you.'

Firing off a fail-safe, get-out-of-jail-free message – 'Hi, signal a bit iffy, arrived safely, about to pick up the pen. x'

Douglas got out of bed. He unpacked his notebooks, pens, research notes and laptop and spread them out on the dining room table. The meadow flowers swayed and nodded as the writer's den was constructed. A quick shower, breakfast and a huge mug of coffee and Douglas was ready to begin.

As always, he read through the last section he'd written and then typed it up. Editing as he went, he sheared off words, added contours and adapted the landscape of his fictional world. Typing up complete, Douglas waited for the next phase of the story to materialise.

It didn't.

For the first time in years the dreaded writer's block had arrived. Douglas drummed his fingertips on the table in frustration. He'd come all this way so he could write and now his brain wasn't co-operating. Pushing the chair back, he paced the room repeating ideas and random phrases out loud. Still nothing.

What a waste of time! He'd come to the back of beyond for nothing. He wasn't even a huge fan of the countryside but, he had a book to finish and a partner to appease. He pulled on his shoes, grabbed his jacket and headed for the door. Maybe this precious country air everyone raved about would give him a starting point.

It was still early and amazingly peaceful as he stepped through the gate and into the meadow. The grasses and wildflowers rustled, parted and welcomed him in. In years to come, Douglas could never really say when the change had come over him. He just knew it had started in that meadow.

The colours from the flowers reached out to him. The vibrant red of the wild poppies clashed beautifully with the bright blue cornflowers. Dotted in between were tiny yellow flowers he couldn't name. The hypnotic hum of bees and insects filled his ears. Butterflies swooped in from all directions. Cabbage Whites danced with Painted Ladies, Red Admirals and other species he didn't know. The sea murmured from over the edge of the cliff and the seagulls circled overhead. Even they sounded joyous. Nature was putting on her best show for him and he couldn't help but respond.

Douglas rocked to a stop and feeling relaxed for the first time in years, he lay down on the springy flowers and grasses. They tickled his neck and ankles, but he didn't mind. He turned his face to the sun. It felt good to feel the rays on his cheeks. They reminded him of Fletcher's kisses - warm and tender.

Fletcher – the one who had always believed in him and encouraged him to keep writing. The one who made sure he ate properly and looked after himself. The one constant in his life for the last twenty years. Fletcher, who he'd most definitely started to take for granted.

Opening his eyes, he thought back to some of the things he'd done and said over the last couple of years and bit his lip. Sitting up, he looked across the bobbing flowers and felt ashamed. He'd be lost without Fletcher. Utterly lost.

Who else would he bounce ideas off? Who would give him the reassurance that all creatives needed when the terrible seed of self-doubt plants itself deep inside the brain? Who else would remind him to empty the bin or clean the bathroom?

What was it Fletcher had said? 'We need to talk about us'? Dear God, he wasn't thinking of leaving, was he? Douglas stared at the beautiful landscape around him which would mean nothing if he couldn't tell Fletcher about it. He stood up and ran full pelt back through the meadow. Flowers and grasses were parted, pushed over and crushed beneath his feet. He ran on.

Back at the cottage he grabbed his phone from the bedside table and called Fletcher.

The phone rang out and with each ring Douglas' stomach clenched with fear and dread until finally...

'Hi Doug, thought you'd be head-down in plots and characters.' Fletcher's familiar voice filled his ears and he felt grounded.

'Look don't worry about that. This is important.' His voice was ragged from running.

'I'm all ears, fire away,' said Fletcher.

'Any chance you can get a train down here and join me?'

'Really?' The surprise in Fletcher's voice cut Douglas to the quick. 'Won't I be in the way? Mr Mackerel will be demanding your full attention surely?'

'Forget Jack bloody Mackerel, I really want to see you. I know I've been an idiot lately.'

'What's brought this on?' Fletcher's surprise had grown.

'Let's just say, I've had my eyes opened by Mother Nature. Look, I need to put things right. I need to put us right. I love you and I want you to come and join me. Will you?'

'Well how can a guy refuse an offer like that?' Fletcher's voice, while still surprised, sounded jubilant too. 'I'll check the train times and get back to you.'

'Whatever time, it doesn't matter. Just book a train and I'll come and pick you up.'

'Thanks Doug. And thank you for remembering us. I'll ring you later.'

Douglas hung up and smiled. He took his shoes off and placed them neatly by the wall. Next he took his coat off and hung it in its proper place on the coat rack by the front door. He walked back into the dining room, sat down and started to write.

ACKNOWLEDGEMENTS

The name on the front cover may be mine but there are a whole cast of people who have helped to make this book possible.

I'm truly thankful to –
My lovely friend and editor Sue Miller plus everyone at Team Author UK who have helped put the book together and made the publishing process as straightforward as possible.

Michelle Catanach for the brilliant front cover and to my dad Paul and brother Lenny who are always so supportive. Special thanks to my partner Dom who always believes in me.

My BETA readers – Bob Stone, Cath Roberts, Jeanette Moore and Lexi Rees who gave such invaluable feedback about my stories. I listened to them, took on board their comments, made some changes and hopefully this is reflected in the final collection.

My fabulous writing group, The Revolting Peasants. It's down to them that my pen has deviated from the path of children's stories and discovered the delights of writing for grown-ups.

Thanks also to Bob Stone and Fran Walker whose combined brain power came up with the perfect title for this book.

Thanks to you dear reader. Thanks for picking my book from the thousands that are available. If you've enjoyed it, I'd really appreciate it if you could leave a review on my Facebook page or on Amazon.

ABOUT THE AUTHOR

Jude is a former Primary and Early Years teacher who left the chalk dust behind to become a professional storyteller (Little Lamb Tales) and author. She published her first children's book, The Dragon of Allerton Oak in 2015. Her storytelling mascot Lamby also features in his own series of books along with the rest of the storytelling mascots aka Team Lamby.

Jude loves collaborating and has worked closely with The Bobby Colleran Trust, The Happiness Club, and Hal's Books to produce books with messages about road safety, Mindfulness for children and Autism Awareness respectively.

A Slice of Lennon is her first venture into writing for adults but hopefully not her last. A full-blown novel is waiting for her to finish planning, stop procrastinating and write it.

When she isn't reading, writing or researching stories, Jude loves to go camping in her vintage VW van Buttercup who also features in one of her books. She's also a fan of walking, beaches, music and gin. She lives with her partner Dom in Liverpool. A musician and a writer in the same house means that the dusting doesn't always get done
but there is creativity aplenty.

For more information please visit:
www.littlelambpublishing.co.uk

Follow Jude on Social Media:

F: @JudeLennonAuthor
T: @JudeLennonBooks
I: @JudeLennonBooks

Printed in Great Britain
by Amazon

42931741R00054